D0951893

I CAN MAKE THIS PROMISE

I CAN MAKE THIS PROMISE

CHRISTINE DAY

HARPER

An Imprint of HarperCollinsPublishers

Library of Congress Cataloging-in-Publication Data

Names: Day, Christine, author.
Title: I can make this promise / Christine Day.
Description: New York, NY : HarperCollins, 2019. | Summary: "When
    twelve-year-old Edie finds letters and photographs in her attic that
    change everything she thought she knew about her Native American
    mother's adoption, she realizes she has a lot to learn about her family's
    history and her own identity"-- Provided by publisher.
Identifiers: LCCN 2019009519 | ISBN 978-0-06-287199-2 (hardback)
Subjects: | CYAC: Identity—Fiction. | Family life—Washington
    (State)—Seattle—Fiction. | Secrets—Fiction. | Coast Salish Indians—
    Fiction. | Indians of North America—Washington (State)—Fiction.
    | Adoption—Fiction. | Seattle (Wash.)—Fiction. | BISAC: JUVENILE
    FICTION / Family / Adoption. | JUVENILE FICTION / People &
    Places / United States / Native American. | JUVENILE FICTION /
    Social Issues / Prejudice & Racism.
Classification: LCC PZ7.1.D392 Iaf 2019 | DDC [Fic]--dc23 LC record
    available at https://lccn.loc.gov/2019009519

Typography by Sarah Nichole Kaufman
19 20 21 22 23   PC/LSCH   10 9 8 7 6 5 4 3 2 1
❖
First Edition

*For the grandmothers and
mothers who came before me.*

PROLOGUE
WHERE ARE YOU FROM?

I never thought of myself as "different" until my first day of kindergarten.

I remember round tables with flimsy tops, plastic chairs with shiny metal legs. Books and stuffed animals were gathered around a fake tree in the reading corner. Cloud-shaped mobiles hung from the ceiling, strands of paper raindrops suspended in midair. A bright yellow sun was painted across one wall. The alphabet was spelled out in a rainbow of uppercase letters.

My classmates already seemed to know each

other. Everyone was talking and laughing and shouting. I was one of the tallest people in the room, but I felt invisible. I didn't know how to join the conversations, the noise. I wasn't even sure if I wanted to.

Mrs. Vespucci saw me, hovering near the classroom door. She hurried over and knelt before me. Her smile revealed straight, white teeth. She reminded me of a fairy-tale princess. Her voice was like a melody, her hair like spun gold. I imagined her singing lullabies to an audience of fawns and bluebirds.

"Hello, Edith."

A jolt of surprise, before I remembered my name tag. A school-issued lanyard was looped around my neck, clipped to a laminated square: *Edith* with an illustrated elephant. *E* for elephant, *E* for me.

"Wow." The teacher's grin widened as she stared at my face. "What are you?"

I told her, "I'm Edie."

"Oh, Edie? That's your preferred name? Where are you from, sweetheart? You're such a pretty girl."

"I live in Seattle."

"Yes, that's true. But where are you *originally* from?"

"Seattle?"

Mrs. Vespucci laughed, but I wasn't sure what was funny. "Do you know where your parents lived before they came here?"

Her questions made me feel panicked. This was my first test, and somehow, I was failing. I couldn't speak. I didn't understand what she was asking. I didn't know what she wanted from me.

I've gotten the question a lot since then: "What are you? Where are you from?"

What am I?

My father is American, and my mother is Native American.

Technically, Dad has roots in Germany, England, and Wales. But I don't mention this, because it feels dishonest. I've never visited these places. I don't know much about them. I'm not even sure where they are in the European continent.

So I just say Dad is American. Which works out fine, because no one asks about him anyways. They jump straight to Mom. They want to know what it means to be Native American.

They ask me what tribe I'm from. They ask if I know what buffalo tastes like. They ask about my spiritual beliefs. They ask about the percentages and ratios of my blood.

My answer remains the same: "I don't really know. My mom was adopted."

1.

THE BIG BANG

July 4

Fireworks are banned in my neighborhood. There are too many trees, too many houses. So this year for the Fourth of July, my parents are taking me to the Tulalip reservation, about twenty miles north of the city. They sell all kinds of fireworks, and they have a huge field where you can set them off. This place is crowded and colorful and chaotic. It's amazing.

My parents lead the way to the booths. There's a food truck parked beside the big gravel lot, selling authentic Mexican tacos. The smell of cooked, seasoned meat fills the air, mixing with the peppery gunpowder from all the fireworks. I can practically *feel* it, in little flecks of grime all over my skin.

Mom asks, "Do you need these, Edie?" She opens her palm, revealing a little package of earplugs.

I shake my head. "I'm okay, thanks."

The booths are set up in several rows. The nearest one is decorated with red, white, and blue streamers, and a huge banner that shouts "FIRE-WORKS" in bold letters. The booth across from it is lime green, with little alien heads and UFOs outlined all over it in black paint. Another is hot pink, with candy-colored rockets arranged in bouquets on its counter. The next is blue, with the Seattle Seahawks logo stenciled in stark white and silver, plus the number 12; the 1 is shaped like the Space Needle.

I like this graffiti. I like the bright colors, the bold lines. I wonder if they created drawings and stencils first, or if they just grabbed their cans of spray paint and improvised. I also wonder if they keep sketchbooks, or have favorite places to draw, like I do. I'm always curious about other artists and their habits, their unfinished drafts, their inspirations.

As we keep moving, I can't help but drink it all in. I've never been to a reservation before. Each person I make eye contact with feels significant. It's possible some of them are distant relatives. I could be walking past cousins or aunties right now, and I wouldn't even know it.

A rock-and-roll version of "The Star-Spangled Banner" starts blaring out of nowhere, and I glance around myself, trying to find the speakers. But as the loud electric guitar mimics the sounds of "O say, can you see?" I instead notice a food vendor with signs that say they have traditional Native American fry bread.

I stop and stare. The line is huge. The menu is handwritten on a whiteboard. An ice-filled cooler contains sodas and bottled lemonades. There are two open counters—one where you pay, one where you wait for your order. I watch as a girl receives her food. The fry bread is a rumpled, golden-brown disk, served on a paper plate. It almost looks like an elephant ear.

As the guitar transitions to a choppy "What so proudly we hailed—" something knocks into the backs of my legs. I stumble and turn around. A dog peers up at me with watery, bloodshot eyes. He's panting hard, and his fur is mangy, but he looks happy. Surprisingly calm. I thought all dogs hated fireworks, but he doesn't seem to mind the noise, the chaos. He just looks a little lost.

I extend my hand to him. "Hi, puppy."

He lifts his big nose. Sniffs my fingers. Pushes his snout against my palm. His tail wags ferociously as he inches closer.

"That's a good boy," I say. "You're a good boy."

I check his neck, but he isn't wearing a collar.

I glance around. Cash registers chime, and shouts of laughter are eclipsed by a huge *boom*. Shoes crunch across the gravel. A group of men walk by in mismatched basketball jerseys. A teenager adjusts her sunglasses; her colorful, beaded bracelets slide down her brown forearm. A guy with two long, dark braids is wearing a Batman tank top. A toddler is mid-meltdown, hands clamped over her ears, face crumpled as she cries out.

"Poor thing," I murmur. I stroke the dog's head, distracted. "Where's your owner?"

The rock-and-roll version of "The Star-Spangled Banner" is no longer recognizable. The guitar riffs have dissolved into wails. It doesn't sound like "O'er the ramparts we watched." It doesn't sound like anything. Just crashing notes and frantic energy.

I turn in the other direction, and an older woman catches my gaze and holds it. She's seated on a stool at the edge of the crowd. Her T-shirt bears the message "Find Our Missing Girls." Huh. I wonder what that's about.

"Edie?" Mom's voice cuts in through the blaring guitar and blasting fireworks. "What are you doing?" She places her hand on my shoulder and gently steers me away. "Honey, you can't pet random dogs like that. It's not safe. Look at how big he is. He might hurt you."

Dad's behind her. "Your mother's right. I know he's cute, but you need to be careful."

"But he's alone," I say. "Shouldn't we help him find his way home?"

"Someone will come along for him," Mom says, and I can barely hear her as the guitar screeches. "Don't worry."

She tugs me away, but I look back. The dog sits in the middle of the walkway. His ears perk up, and his tongue lolls out of the corner of his mouth as he watches me leave.

• • •

We stop at a booth called the Big Bang. The words are spelled out in a swollen graffiti font. The letters are big and puffy and white, and they remind me of squished marshmallows. A brown-skinned teenager stands behind the counter. He's wearing a white tank top, and has a little barbell pierced through his eyebrow.

He grins, as if he's genuinely happy to see us.

"Afternoon, folks." He flicks his chin up in greeting. "How's it going?"

Dad nods in response. "We're doing well, thank you."

A short silence follows as we look around his booth. The top shelf holds the biggest boxes, encased in glossy wrappers. Their labels alternate between sounding patriotic and menacing: "Rocket's Red Glare." "American Outlaw." "Rolling Thunder." "Sabotage." The lower shelves contain smaller boxes and open trays of fireworks.

"Where you guys from?" he asks.

"We live in Seattle," Mom answers.

"Ah." He nods, understanding. "That urban life. You like it out there?"

Mom smiles. "Most of the time."

"Good, good. Glad to hear." He drums his hands

on the countertop. "So what kinds of fireworks are you looking for?"

"I know we want some sparklers, some Roman candles. Maybe a fountain or two?"

"All right." He turns to his lowest shelf and grabs two trays, tilting them forward to reveal their contents. "I have these two kinds," he says. One tray is filled with bundles of slender gray-brown sticks. The other has bundles of hot pink sparklers; the top half of each one is wrapped in dyed magenta-yellow-teal tissue paper and laced with a gold ribbon.

We pick the pretty ones, then select some Roman candles and two stubby fountains. The boy places a long cardboard box on the counter before us and starts piling our stuff inside it.

"Anything else?"

Both my parents look at me. And the boy does, too. I feel heat rise in my cheeks. I go rigid under their scrutiny.

"Edie?" Mom asks. Her voice is gentle, a half whisper at most.

I glance at the shelves and shrug, feeling awkward. I wish she wouldn't have said anything. I hate being put on the spot in front of strangers.

The boy snaps his fingers. "Here," he says. "How 'bout this?"

He crouches behind the counter. I can hear the scrape of crates sliding across the ground. He straightens back up and stands directly across from me, smiling.

"Ever seen one of these before?" He holds up a cylinder, wrapped in a turquoise label. It has a black platform on one end. Its fuse pops out the top like a little red tongue.

I shake my head.

"Really?" He sets it down on the counter. Taps it with his finger. "That's too bad," he says. "These guys are my favorites, out of everything I've got here. That's why I keep 'em hidden. They're reserved for special people." He winks, and now I'm certain my face is all red and splotchy.

"What is it?" I mumble, hoping he'll stop looking at me.

He slides the firework across the counter. "A gift," he says. "A surprise."

I inspect the wrapper, hesitating.

"Go on," he urges. "Take it."

I accept the firework and hold it close against my chest.

"Thank you," Mom says, her voice brimming with gratitude. She retrieves her wallet from the depths of her purse. "How much do I owe you?"

"Twenty-four fifty."

Dad hoists the box into his arms and frowns. "That's a bit low, isn't it?"

"It's all good." The boy inclines his head toward me. "Little sister's is on the house."

My parents protest. They want to pay him the full amount, but he waves their offer away.

He says, "Don't worry about it. Just take care of yourselves out there." And he sounds like he really means it.

2.

THE BOY IN THE WAR ZONE

July 4

It's like a war zone out here in the field.

Whistling fireworks shriek across the sky, long tails of light streaking behind them like shooting stars. The big ones shoot out of their boxes with hollow thumps and explode with echoing claps that set off car alarms. Fountains erupt in glittering sparks, hissing softly as they stand stationary on the ground. The whole meadow is littered with knocked-over tubes and blackened boxes, empty shells that are still venting plumes. The air is smoky and filled with flying bits of debris; there's so much of it, it's almost difficult to breathe.

We've already gone through the entire box. We're standing a respectful distance away from other people. Thickets of trees line the field's perimeter. An explosion goes off, perilously close to a cluster of dry-looking leaves and branches. I swallow and return my attention to our fountain as it huffs blue smoke and embers. Within moments, it fizzles out in a dwindling orange flame.

Dad's hand grazes my shoulder. "Is it time for your mystery firework?"

I nod. "Can I be the one to light it?"

My parents exchange glances. Mom shrugs and nods, granting her permission. Dad says, "Sure. I don't see why not."

He leads me to the spot where our fountain burned out. I set the firework on the ground, and Dad retrieves the lighter from his pocket as we both crouch.

"Just be careful with your fingers," he says. "Don't tilt the flame toward your knuckles. And once the fuse is lit, be sure to back away quick."

"I'm twelve," I tell him. "Not two. Stop worrying so much."

He laughs. "Yeah, well. I guess I should be

grateful you even asked. When I was your age, I don't think I waited for permission to do anything. Especially when it came to fireworks."

I can't help but smirk. Dad's stories often fit into one of two categories: he either talks about Boy Scouts, Little League, and his top grades in math and science; or he talks about mischief, the pranks he used to pull, the hospital trips when daring stunts didn't go well.

It's hard to imagine that some of his stories really happened. But maybe that's because I've only known him since he became a dad.

He hands me the lighter, and I throw a quick glance at Mom. She responds with one of her warmest smiles. The kind that makes her pupils shine and her eyes crinkle around the corners.

Mom doesn't share many of her childhood memories. She doesn't have endless nostalgic stories like Dad does. I know she was smart and shy and liked to read books. I know she and Uncle Phil didn't get along until they were teenagers. I know she was a writer for her high school's newspaper. But that's pretty much it.

"Well?" Dad says. "What are you waiting for?"

I light the fuse. We both stand and back away

swiftly. His arm crosses in front of me protectively. Mom's warm hands grip my shoulders as we watch the fuse disintegrate into nothing.

It goes off with a small *pop!* Something shoots up and out of it, so fast it's just a blur. I throw my head back, amazed by how high it goes, how far it *flies*.

"What is it?" I cry.

Mom gives my shoulders a reassuring squeeze. "Just wait. You'll see."

It's hanging in the sky, floating weightlessly. It isn't burning or shooting sparks. It isn't like any of the other fireworks.

I gasp. "It's a parachute."

It looks like a tiny hot-air balloon. It's striped: turquoise and white. It flutters and flaps as it sails toward the earth, coming down in a diagonal line, heading toward—

The open field.

Horrified, I break free of my mother's grasp.

"Edie!"

Before she can say anything else, I'm running straight across the minefield, dodging around people, charging through the cross fire. I keep my eyes glued to the little parachute as it meanders through the dangerous atmosphere. It looks far too innocent amid the showers of sparks.

I chase it halfway across the field. When it's only about fifteen feet off the ground, I see a boy aiming his Roman candle in the same direction.

"No!" I shout. "Wait!"

The boy turns his head and pivots his body just in time; the Roman candle's projectile misses my parachute by several feet.

I'm completely out of breath now. I slow to a stop and catch the parachute in midair. There's a little cardboard tube attached to it, connected with thin white strings. The striped parachute wrinkles and deflates in my hands.

"Hey!"

I look up. The boy with the Roman candle is staring at me. He's wearing a backward-facing baseball cap. A tuft of his black hair is sticking through the open gap. He's also wearing a black T-shirt and basketball shorts. He looks like he's around my age.

"Sorry," he says with a grimace. "I wasn't trying to point at your parachute."

A green fireball shoots out of his Roman candle with a muted *thunk*. He doesn't bother to watch it arc through the air.

"It's okay."

A blue fireball shoots out of his candle, and he still doesn't look away.

"I'm Roger," he says. He takes a step closer and holds his free hand out to me.

It seems odd to introduce myself to a boy in the middle of a war zone. But I accept the handshake anyway. "Edie."

His palm is warm and soft. A purple fireball erupts from his candle, but I only see it in my peripheral vision, because we're face-to-face now. His eyes are the warmest shade of brown I've ever seen. His teeth are a bright white flash as he smiles at me.

Butterflies surge in my stomach. My blush warms my cheeks.

He says, "Hi."

He's still smiling. His hand is still folded in mine.

"Hi."

"You look Native," he says. "But I don't think I've ever seen you before. What nation are you?"

I blink fast and stutter, "Oh. I mean, yes, I'm Native, b-but—"

"Edie?"

I drop Roger's hand like a hot potato.

Two silhouettes are moving through the thick gray fog. Bits of debris and shrapnel rain around them, like the little black spots that appear on-screen in old movies. As they come closer, I can see the relief on my parents' faces.

"Oh good," Dad mutters. "Sweetheart, you can't just run off like that, okay? Come on, let's go, it's getting late." As an afterthought he adds, "I'm glad you got your parachute."

I respond with a mute nod and speed-walk away from Roger. My parents lead the way back across the field. I follow a few steps behind and risk a quick glance at Roger before he disappears in the fog.

He's staring after me. His Roman candle is still poised in the air, but the tube is smoking, empty.

I lift my hand in a wave.

He smiles as he waves back.

My parents and I are in the car now, zooming down the freeway. Fireworks bloom all along the darkened hillsides. The sky is like a swath of indigo velvet.

I'm still thinking about the dog I saw. I wonder if he ever found his owners, his family. I hope someone was there for him. I hope he's curled up in front of a fireplace right now, with a full belly and a cozy rug. Or maybe he's standing in a bathtub, his tail whacking the tiled walls behind him, his fur lathered in fragrant bubbles.

Actually, these are some great images. Maybe this could be the topic of the story for the film Amelia, Serenity, and I are working on.

I whisk my phone out of my pocket and open our group chat. Happy 4th of July, I type. Movie meeting tomorrow? I got a new idea.

Serenity's response is instant: happy fourth! yes, can't wait. where should we meet?

I ask, Amelia's house?

I stare at the screen for a moment, waiting for Amelia's response. When it doesn't come, I tuck the phone back into my pocket.

Maybe it's only my imagination, but it seems like Amelia takes forever to reply these days. Sometimes, she doesn't even answer at all. Since the summer began, the group chat has mainly been filled with messages exchanged between me and Serenity.

Mom giggles. "Look," she says. She turns around and shows me her phone screen. "Phil just sent me this."

Uncle Phil sent Mom two GIFs and a text message. The first is a fireworks GIF, the second is a wavering American flag. The text reads, Happy Fourth to my favorite sister, my favorite bro-in-law, and my favorite niece! Love you all (but especially Edie). Excited to see you soon for summer BBQs.

"Nice," I say.

"Yes," she agrees. "Very sweet." Mom turns back around and starts typing her response.

"Hey, Mom?"

"Hmm?"

"Why are fireworks only allowed on the reservation?"

She stops typing. Looks up. I meet her gaze in the rearview mirror.

"I was just thinking," I say. "About how fireworks are banned in our neighborhood, because of all the fire hazards. But there are still a lot of trees around that field. And there were houses nearby, too. And it wasn't just, like, one or two houses. There were a bunch of them." I scoot forward in my seat. "So why is it allowed there? Why don't the same rules apply?"

She doesn't answer, at first. I wait and listen to the ongoing *whoosh* of cars on the freeway around us. The dingy bellow of a truck's diesel exhaust. The low, distant wail of sirens.

Finally, she responds with "It's complicated."

I wait for her to explain; she doesn't.

"Have you ever heard of fry bread?"

"Yes. Why?"

"Have you ever tried it?"

"A few times."

"Really?" I scoot even further, straining against the seat belt. "Do you know how to make it? What are the ingredients? Could we cook it at home? They were selling some at a booth, and I wanted to try it but didn't get a chance to ask."

"Maybe we can make it at home. I don't know. We'll see."

"It's a traditional Native American food," I say excitedly. "We *should* make it at home."

"Maybe."

I lean back in my seat. The freeway curves around a bend. Bright white headlights gather behind us, around us. Their beams pierce the dark, illuminating the interior of our car in shifting strobes. Red taillights glow ahead, as we follow them home.

I think about Roger. He was the first person to ever say those words to me. *You look Native.* And it didn't feel presumptuous. It didn't feel like a wild guess.

It was like he recognized me. Like he saw something in me.

I wonder what that something was.

3.

THREE'S COMPANY

July 5

Amelia finally texts back the next morning, at 9:34 a.m. She says, My house is fine.

I'm sitting in the backyard with my drawing pad in my lap while Mom works in the garden, padding its perimeter with bark chips and seaweed. Seaweed is the secret behind her green thumb; she calls it Mother Nature's Slug Repellent. Her flowers burst with color and fragrance. There are lush pink peonies, their petals delicately ruffled, like the folds of a tulle tutu. Sunset-colored dahlias, blooming atop slender green stems. And countless other blossoms and spikes of herbs I can't name.

The morning sunshine is warm against my hair, my skin. I'm sketching an outline of this one flower in the garden. Its blooms are my favorite shade of purple: bright and soft, like lilac but not. Its petals are spread out in the shape of a star. Little yellow sprigs pop up from its pollen-filled middle.

A new message from Serenity: **wow took u long enough! what time can we head over?**

Seriously. I was starting to wonder if we'd even see each other today.

I have some drawings ready to share with them. I worked on them last night, after we came home. The dog from the reservation now appears across several pages in my drawing pad, in various positions: seated, sleeping, running, and carefree with a stick in his mouth. I've also drawn him into a few settings: sitting in the middle of the fireworks stands, in the forest, on the beach.

I feel like I should name him. But I don't know what name to choose.

My phone buzzes again: **Come over at 11.**

Excellent, I type back.

This is good news. We really need to get to work, since we're going to enter the festival this summer.

"Is that Amelia and Serenity?" Mom asks.

"Yep." I set my phone aside. Pick up the drawing pencil. "We're hanging out soon."

"Are they coming over?"

"We're meeting at Amelia's house."

"Fun, fun." Mom stands up. Brushes her gloved hands together, raining flecks of dirt all over the grass. "Can I see what you're working on?"

"Sure."

I erase the tip of a petal and redo it with a softer sweep. Some of the lines I've drawn are too sharp, too angular. The flowers I'm trying to capture are more delicate than this. I can imagine what Mrs. Barnes—my art teacher—would say, if she were here: *Follow the lines, Edie. Don't put too much pressure on your pencil. Just follow the lines, light and natural.*

Mom, on the other hand, is never critical of my work. She peers down at the open page and declares, "Perfection."

It's not perfect, but I smile and thank her anyways.

It's too noisy to talk inside Amelia's house. Her little brother, Adam, is smashing his Legos and watching cartoons at top volume in the living room. And Amelia's mom is vacuuming upstairs, the clunky machine roaring across the carpets.

So we're in the backyard, lying on the black woven surface of her trampoline. Serenity is examining my drawing pad, her brows furrowed in concentration. Amelia is flat on her back, her eyes unfocused, long blonde hair fanned around her head.

"These are great, Edie." Serenity touches the mangy, graphite-sketched fur. "I love it."

"Thanks," I say. "We need a name for him."

"He looks like a Bruno to me."

"Bruno! That totally fits him."

She gestures to Amelia. "Wanna see?"

Amelia sighs and lifts herself up onto her elbows. "'Kay." She takes it, gives it a quick glance. "I like the drawings," she says. "But this story is played out, don't you think? The lost dog, looking for a home. A million of these movies already exist."

"We can still make it our own," Serenity says. "And besides, it's not like we're going to Hollywood. This is for a youth filmmaking festival. It's small and local and people would love this story."

"Exactly," I chime in. "It's about a dog. Everybody loves dogs."

"Yes!" Serenity says. "Except for people who are allergic to them. Obviously."

Amelia shrugs, unimpressed. "I just think we can aim higher. That's all."

Serenity and I exchange uneasy glances. Amelia is acting weird today. We don't know what's up with her.

"Okay," I say, treading carefully. "Well. We can keep brainstorming."

I reach for my drawing pad, and she gives it back. I flip through the numerous pages I've filled with this dog. I thought for sure they'd both fall in love with him.

"We can go back to the Rapunzel-inspired story," Serenity suggests. "The princess trapped in a tower."

"But that's cliché and overdone, too."

I bite my lip. "I'd rather keep an animal as our main character," I say. "I'm not the best at drawing people, remember?"

I'm way more comfortable with drawing creatures, plants, landscapes. The stuff you find in nature. I'm not nearly as good with human portraits. My faces tend to come out lopsided. The bodies I draw always look stiff and awkward. And hands are the hardest part of all. I can't help but draw them with crooked fingers, weirdly shaped palms, or unnatural bends to the wrists.

Mrs. Barnes tried to help me with this, in our after-school art club. But even with her guidance, I lost patience for it. I know what I'm good at, and I know what I suck at.

I suck at illustrating people.

"Why don't we shoot our own footage and act it out, like everyone else?" Amelia asks.

"Because my dad already downloaded the animation software," I tell her. "We couldn't change our minds after he did that for us."

This whole plan has been in motion for a while now. Amelia is the director and lead vocal talent, Serenity is the screenwriter and side vocals, and I'm the animator.

"But the animation is making this ten times harder than it needs to be."

"We're challenging ourselves," I say optimistically. "And it will make our film the most unique."

Amelia scrunches her nose. "Fine. We'll figure it out later, I guess." She flops back on the trampoline, and we all bounce slightly with her shifting weight. "You know what sounds incredible right now?"

"What?"

"A Popsicle."

"Ooh," Serenity says. "That sounds *amazing*."

"Too bad Adam ate our last one yesterday."

An idea pops up in my head. "Hey, you know what we could do? We could go to my house and make our *own* Popsicles."

My two best friends gawk at me.

"You know how to make your own Popsicles?" Amelia asks. Her voice is a little scornful, like she's mad at me for withholding this information.

"My mom bought a Popsicle mold last year, at the end of the summer," I explain. "We only used it once, but it was awesome. We used real fruit and berries."

For the first time today, Amelia beams at me. She nods and says she loves the idea; she insists that we leave immediately.

Finally, all three of us agree on something. I feel triumphant as we leave the trampoline, but also a little concerned. Something is up that she's not telling me.

4.

A STRANGER SO FAMILIAR

July 5

"Are you sure we should be doing this without telling your mom?" Serenity asks as I lower the attic door and unfold its ladder.

"It's fine," I say. "She won't mind."

The Popsicle molds weren't in the freezer, and we couldn't find them anywhere else in the kitchen, so I reasoned they had to be up here. And Mom didn't respond to us at all when we came in through the front door. She's probably still gardening in the backyard.

"But we could ask her where they are," Amelia

says. "She'll probably know for sure."

"If we don't find them on our own, we'll ask her."

I motion for them to follow as I climb the short ladder and crawl into the attic. It's stuffy and hot in here. And surprisingly dark, despite the midday sun streaming through the square window. Bare wooden beams form triangles that hold up the ceiling. Cardboard boxes and plastic storage bins are stacked everywhere in haphazard piles. An old computer monitor gazes up at me from its spot on the floor. Its black screen is bloated and curved, and its boxy white backside is propped against a dartboard. It's the fattest computer I've ever seen.

"Whoa," Amelia whispers as she emerges through the attic door. "There's so much stuff up here."

"Yeah," I murmur as I look around. "I haven't been up here in ages."

Serenity crawls in next, and immediately points at the computer. "What the heck?" she says. "That's a *huge* computer."

"Vintage," Amelia agrees. "Super weird."

All three of us stand and stare around the space. The storage bins are stacked in small towers. The cardboard boxes are bulging and worn. I see a rolled-up newspaper, a collection of picture books I read when I was little, a bin filled with Christmas lights in tangled clusters. A box of souvenirs from Disneyland, including Minnie Mouse ears with my full name embroidered on them.

My friends and I move in different directions. For some reason, we tiptoe across the floor and peek inside boxes with slow, careful movements. I'm not sure where this urge to be quiet is coming from, but we all seem to feel it. There's something about this place. Something about this tiny room.

"Edie?"

"Yeah?"

Serenity is staring at me, squinting like she's trying to solve a puzzle or a difficult math equation. "Could you come here for a sec?"

I frown. "Sure."

I make my way toward her, meandering through the narrow path, stepping over the clutter.

"What's going on?" Amelia asks.

Serenity waves her over. "You come look at this, too." Then she holds her hand up, stopping me. "Wait right there, Edie. I want to see something."

My frown deepens. "What are you talking about?"

Amelia reaches her side, and Serenity holds up a large white rectangle. A photograph. She extends her arm, keeping it in their line of sight, as they both face me.

"Do you see what I see?" Serenity asks.

Amelia stares for three full seconds before she says, "Oh. My. God."

Together, they both look up at me. I can actually see their pupils dilating.

"What?" I snap. "Why are you looking at me like that?"

"Edie," Serenity says. "Do you know who this is?"

She flips the photograph to face me.

I squint at it. Take a step closer.

"No," I say, because I've never seen this picture before. It's a black-and-white modeling head shot. A young woman gazes at the camera, her head tilted at a slight angle. She has dark hair, cut in a short, fluffy bob. She's standing in front of a white wall. And she's smiling.

It's the smile that makes me stop short. It's the smile that makes me look a little closer.

I've never seen her before. I'm still certain of that. And yet, her face is so . . . *familiar*. My mind is scrolling, trying to place where I've seen her before. I feel like I recognize her. Like I *know* her from somewhere.

But I don't make the connection until Serenity voices it.

"She looks like you," she says. "She looks almost exactly like you."

Those words chill me to the bone.

For a split second, the world seems to tilt on its axis, like it's about to roll right off its designated ring in the solar system and float aimlessly into outer space.

She looks like me. She's a complete stranger, but she has my face. Her eyes are shaped like mine. Her nose resembles mine. The apples of her cheeks are pronounced and a little pudgy as she smiles, and she has a gap between her two front teeth. Go downstairs and you'll see a whole hallway lined with photographs featuring that same exact smile. In every one of my school pictures. Every single family portrait.

"Look at this," Serenity urges. "The box I found it in."

She grabs me by the wrist, tugs me forward. It's a cardboard box, marked with a capital *E* in black Sharpie. The top flaps are fraying around the edges, and layered with tape that isn't sticky anymore.

We both drop to our knees before it. I pull the box toward me. Its corners are worn and weak, bending easily beneath my grip.

A manila folder is tucked inside the box, along with loose papers, envelopes with broken seals, postcards with bright illustrations. A notebook with a thick black cover, a swollen middle.

I flip the manila folder open. It's filled with more modeling head shots. Multiple takes of the same poses, including the one Serenity is holding, as well as others. The familiar woman gazes directly at the camera, unsmiling. She looks off somewhere in the distance, her eyes unfocused, faraway. She gives a small, private smile as she glances to the side, her chin tucked down to her shoulder.

"Is she famous?" Amelia asks. "Only actresses and models have head shots like that. Was she an actress?"

"I don't know."

Amelia points past my shoulder. "Those are postcards from California! She *must* have been in Hollywood."

Serenity gasps. *"Edie,"* she wheezes. "Look."

She points into the box. Amelia gasps, too, claps her hands over her mouth. I'm unable to make a sound.

We're staring at an open letter. I reach into the box, carefully lift it up. It's crinkly and thin beneath my fingertips, and lined with several rows of inky cursive.

The date at the top is December 14, 1973.

The message is somewhat short. I skim straight down the paper, seeing these words without really reading them, because the phrase that matters most is penned at the very end.

Two words: *Love, Edith.*

5.

E FOR EDITH, E FOR ME

July 5

"That can't be a coincidence," Serenity says. "Edith isn't a common name."

"For real," Amelia agrees. She glances at me, and I see concern and curiosity in her eyes. "Whoever she is, she must have been important to your parents."

I'm at a loss for words. The letter feels limp in my hands. I've never given my name much thought. I know what it means ("prosperous in war," which has always seemed a bit odd to me). And I know that it's rare, old-fashioned (Libby—the meanest girl in our grade, and possibly the entire school—used to call me "Granny," because she thought Edith was a "grandma name").

But I didn't think my name was an inheritance. My parents have never mentioned any other Ediths. As far as I know, none exist in our family tree.

So who is this woman? Where did this box come from? What does this all mean?

Amelia places a gentle hand on my knee. "It looks like your parents have been keeping secrets from you."

Mom and Uncle Phil aren't related by blood. Grandma and Grandpa Miller brought her home from an orphanage when she was only a few months old. This is the story I know about where Mom came from, and how she fits in with the Millers.

Aside from the fact that she's Native American, of course. That part has never been a secret. But it's never been elaborated on, either.

"Don't you know anything about your mother's biological family?" Serenity leans in, focusing on my face. "Your mom must have learned something about them."

"I think it's safe to say she did. I mean, again"—

Amelia gestures meaningfully at the photographs—"just saying."

I nod. Fold the letter along its creases. Tuck it back inside the box.

Serenity asks, "You okay?"

"Fine." The word sounds false. "I'm fine."

My two friends are watching me closely. They both know how much I wish I had a big family. I have no siblings, no cousins. No aunties to visit in Hawaii or California, like Amelia. No elders to bake cookies with during the holidays, like Serenity. (All of my grandparents had passed by the time I was four years old.) I love my parents and Uncle Phil very much, and I know I'm lucky to have them. Still, I can't help but wonder how different my life would be if I had a little sister to play with, or an older brother to look out for me. Or grandparents or great-somethings, to tell me stories from "the old days."

Where are you from?

A bitter taste fills my mouth. I'm staring at letters and photographs from a woman who potentially could have answered that question. This is proof that my own *parents* might hold the answers.

Why didn't they ever tell me about her? We're

close; we share everything.

Or so I thought.

Amelia asks Serenity, "Is she in shock?"

"I think so," Serenity answers gravely.

And then from downstairs: "Edie? Hello?"

Our eyes widen. All three of us exchange frantic glances.

"Sweetie?" Mom calls from the hallway below. "What are you doing in the attic?"

Amelia grips my shoulder and whispers, "What should we tell her?"

I feel breathless. "I don't know," I say. *It looks like your parents have been keeping secrets from you.* "I don't—" *Your mom must have learned something about them.* I shake my head over and over. "Not this," I squeak. "Something else."

Mom yells, "Edie! Are you up there?"

I can feel my pulse in my neck. "Yes, Mom," I call back. "We're here. We were just—" Amelia's hand tightens on my shoulder; Serenity's eyes widen. I shake my head again, feeling helpless.

Then Amelia shouts, "We were looking for your Popsicle molds, Mrs. Green. Do you know where they are?"

"Oh," Mom says. She gives a small, breathy

laugh. "I know exactly where those are. I stored them in the cupboard above the fridge. Why don't you girls come down, and we'll make some? I have fresh strawberries and blueberries you can use."

Amelia says, "Sounds wonderful, Mrs. Green! Thanks so much, we'll be right down."

"I'll be waiting," Mom says. Her footsteps move down the hall, toward the kitchen.

Amelia releases my shoulder. "You okay?"

I nod. "Thank you."

"I think you did the right thing," Amelia says. "Keep this discovery a secret, at least for now. Serenity and I can help you do some research and go through the box. We'll figure out who this other Edith is on our own."

Serenity glances back and forth between us. "Maybe Edie should be honest with her mom."

I swallow. "My mom wasn't honest with *me*."

"She's right," Amelia says. She eyes the box. "Something's going on here. And if Edie's mom didn't tell the truth before, why would she start now?"

6.

ORIGINS

July 5

The Popsicles are still in the freezer, but my friends are gone. Serenity had to meet her dad. Amelia's mom called her home to do some chores.

And now I'm slumped on the couch, staring at nothing. My drawing pad is open on the coffee table before me, but the page is blank. I don't know where to begin.

Love, Edith.

I want to go back to the attic and read that full letter. I want to learn more about who she was, and how we're . . . *related.* I'm almost certain that we are. What else would explain the resemblance, the shared name, the existence of that box?

There *is* another Edith in my family tree. There are whole roots and branches I've never known before. I want to dig through the dirt, climb through these tangled limbs, inspect this gnarled trunk. I want to see who she is to me. I want to learn the names of who else was here.

Dad's home from work. He has a bag of fast food clutched in one fist as he comes through the front door; the other grips his keys, which he yanks free from the doorknob.

His hair is mussed, his necktie is loose, and he's already shrugging out of his sport coat. He wears fancy clothes to work, but I know he hates them. He looks like he can never take a deep breath in these outfits.

"Hey, sweetie," he says. "How was your day?"

"Interesting." I keep my voice vague. "How was yours?"

"Long," he says. Which is always his answer after a full day of work. "Come eat dinner."

I follow him into the dining room, where he and Mom hug and greet each other. Her hands slide up and down his back. He presses a quick kiss to the top of her head. And they seem so sweet, so happy. Like they couldn't possibly have anything to hide. Especially not from their only daughter.

The chair legs scrape as I drop into my seat at the table, and my parents soon follow.

Mom gives me a friendly smile as she sits. "Hungry, sweetie?"

I shrug in response.

Dad's sport coat is gone, his necktie has been tossed aside, and his crisp white sleeves are now rolled up to his elbows. He retrieves a foil-wrapped burger from the grease-spotted bag.

"You know"— he groans as he sinks into his chair—"I really hate going back to work after holidays. It's the worst feeling ever." The foil crinkles as he pries the layers apart. "I should've become a math teacher. Then I'd have whole summers off, just me and my girls. Wouldn't that be neat?" He brushes away some loose shreds of lettuce. Takes the burger in his hands, props his elbows up on the table. "Imagine all the great stuff we could do if I didn't have to work all the time."

The clock on the wall *tick-tick-tick*s in a brisk, even beat. A bead of condensation drips down the side of my milkshake, settling at the base of the plastic cup. A warm breeze wafts through the open windows behind my parents, shifting the white cotton curtains.

"Maybe I could get a job," Mom offers gingerly. "And you could take some well-deserved time off."

I slurp at my milkshake. Dad shakes his head, swallows his mouthful with a forced gulp.

"No way," he says. "I mean, if that's what you wanted, you absolutely could. But please don't let me guilt you into thinking you should work outside the home. I know I complain sometimes, but really, I wouldn't change a thing about our situation. I'm happy to support my family."

Mom flushes. Smiles down at her chicken burger. "And I love being a stay-at-home mom. Despite the weird politics at PTA meetings."

A short silence follows as we all dive into our meals.

Then Dad crunches a french fry and says, "When we learned your mother was pregnant, that was one of the first decisions she made. She quit her job and didn't look back. She knew that raising a child is the most important work in the world, and she wanted to dedicate all her time and energy to you."

My heart gives a subtle thud.

Honestly, this isn't unusual. My parents always share stories and memories about me as a toddler, a baby, a "bun in the oven."

But they've never shared where my name came from.

Not once.

"Well," Mom says. "It's also a tremendous privilege, to be a full-time parent. Not all mothers or fathers get the chance to do this."

"True." Dad's voice goes soft and solemn. "That's very true."

I drag a french fry through some ketchup. My stomach feels too queasy to eat a full burger right now. I'm stalling with tiny nibbles.

"Edie," Dad says. "Is everything okay? You're quiet tonight."

Another breeze whispers through the windows, fluttering the curtains.

"Yeah, I'm fine. Just thinking."

"About?"

I clasp my milkshake, draw out the silence with a long, cold sip. Mom and Dad wait and watch me without touching their own food. Finally, I swallow and sit up.

"I guess I'm just wondering where, um—where my name came from?"

Dad gives the smallest flinch. Mom's face doesn't move; she doesn't seem to breathe.

"Why am I Edith?" I ask. "Why not Emily, or Ella? Where did—" I breathe in. Brace myself. "Where did my name come from?"

For a second, it's as if my parents have turned to stone.

They sit with stiff, awkward postures. Their gazes turn distant, faraway.

"And it's so old-fashioned," I add. "I don't know any other Ediths."

Dad blinks. Focuses his attention on Mom, even as he asks me, "Where's this coming from, sweetie? Is that girl from school bothering you again?"

Now it's my turn to flinch. I forgot I told my parents about Libby's teasing.

"No," I say. My face burns as I spin a quick lie from half-truths: "Amelia and I were talking earlier about how she was named after her mom's favorite aunt. And Serenity said she was named after a prayer. They both wanted to know where my name came from, and I didn't know what to tell them."

I can't look at either of my parents as I say this.

Mom laughs, but it comes out airy and strange. "Well, honey. You have a vintage name. It's classic. Timeless."

My stomach plummets. "Is that why you chose it? Because it was . . . *vintage?*"

She shrugs. "We gave you a name you could grow into. Something meaningful."

"So, you wanted me to be 'prosperous in war'? That's the literal meaning of it."

"Not necessarily, just—" She waves one hand. Squints at the tabletop. "Prosperous. Happy. Despite anything and everything that gets in your way."

"Huh."

"You haven't touched your burger, Edie. Eat."

I take a mechanical bite and chew without tasting.

My mother just lied to me, so easily. Like it cost her nothing.

7.

GOLDEN GARDENS

July 5

We go to Golden Gardens after dinner, which only makes their guilt more obvious. There are certain things my parents do whenever something is wrong and they want to make me feel better: they feed me tons of sugar, they buy me new art supplies, or they take me here.

Golden Gardens is my favorite park in Seattle, and my favorite place to draw. It's a public beach on the Puget Sound waterfront, with concrete trails and grassy picnic areas, huge stretches of sand littered with driftwood logs and chipped seashells.

Beach towels are strewn across the lumpy sea-shore, striped umbrellas and plastic pails anchored beside them. Dogs crash into the water, splashing as they chase after sticks.

My drawing pad is open in my lap. I'm trying to focus on my work, following the lines across the horizon. I draw a little splash mark into one corner of the beach, with a shaggy form diving into it. I imagine Bruno here, running and playing like all the other dogs. I remember the soft pressure of his nose against my palm. His tongue lolling to the side as he watched me walk away.

Maybe I shouldn't have walked away.

Somewhere in the distance, a ferry blasts its horn. The wind picks up, fluttering the pages of my pad, revealing the drawing of that purple flower in my mother's garden. The sight of it frustrates me so much, I flip the page back too hard and accidentally rip its corner.

I breathe in through my nose, out through my mouth. I touch my pencil to the paper, willing myself to focus, to follow the ripples of light across the water. The textured tops of the evergreen trees. The rise and fall of the Olympic Mountains.

Why would my mother lie about my name? What's the point of locking the other Edith inside a box in the attic? Who was she, and why was she important? Why is she top secret?

I really don't understand.

And where is she now? How does the adoption factor in?

My phone buzzes in my pocket. I pull it free, unlock the new message.

Serenity: you should ask ur parents about her.

I nearly drop my phone in my haste to hide her words. My parents are sitting on either side of me on the park bench. They're both reading, focused on the open novels in their hands, but you never know. They might try to peek at my messages. I don't know if I can trust them.

I shove the phone deep inside my pocket. Return to my drawing pad.

The tip of my pencil breaks. It leaves an ugly dash across my drawing, right through the middle of a lopsided mountain. It's ruined. Completely ruined.

I snap the sketchbook shut and set it aside with more force than necessary. Mom notices, and I can feel the disturbance in our bubble of silence. But she doesn't say anything, which is fine. I don't want her to.

Indigo mountains line the horizon in jagged

peaks. The sun dips low, and a summit sinks into it like a thorn. Its fragile golden skin is punctured, and the sun bleeds oranges and yellows across the bottom of the sky.

I don't think I'll ever be able to capture something like this. No matter how hard I try.

8.

THE COMPUTER

July 6

Amelia: I have a brilliant idea to share with you. Can we hang out tomorrow?

Me: Sure.

Amelia: Awesome. And wait for me before you go through the box. I want to learn EVERYTHING about the other Edith.

I stare at Amelia's words, conflicted. All night long, the box in the attic called to me, as if an invisible fishing line connected my fingertips to its cardboard edge. I felt a constant tug and pull, this sense that every time I opened my eyes, I was reaching for her through the dark.

Me: You can't come over today?

My thumbs hover over the glowing screen. The phone vibrates in my palm.

Amelia: Sorry, no. Busy. Pretty pleeeeease can we do it tomorrow?!

I sigh. Me: I'll wait for you, but I'm bringing the box down to my room. Don't want us to go back in the attic while my parents are around. They might get suspicious.

She sends me two thumbs-up emojis.

I rise from the living room couch and inch past the doorway to the kitchen.

Mom knocks an egg against the kitchen counter. Its shell splits in two, and the raw yolk drops into the skillet with a slick-sounding *thwick*. Dad pours pale batter over our waffle iron. Bacon is sizzling on the stovetop; the coffeepot is gurgling in its corner. Both my parents are focused on their tasks, speaking to each other in hushed voices.

I hurry down the hall. Rise up on my tiptoes. Lower the ladder. It unfolds with a noisy creak, and I wince, but I don't think either of them heard it.

Still. Need to make this fast.

I climb the ladder, pull myself over the ledge,

dodge around various piles of junk. Scoop the box up in my arms.

Hurry back.

Despite how careful I am, my shoe clips the edge of the fat computer monitor. It topples over with a clunk, screen-first. Then—unbelievably—its boxy rear end tips to the side, and in apparent slow motion, it falls over with an even louder *smash*.

My breath whooshes out of me.

My parents must have heard *that*.

For a split second, I'm frozen, unable to move. Unable to do anything. Then the air rushes back into my lungs, and I set the box aside to crouch and give the monitor a push, rolling the stupid thing to its original spot. But it's heavier than it looks, and I'm struggling with it, clenching my teeth as it clunks in place.

Relieved, I stand and step back. Reach for the box.

Freeze.

No. No, this isn't right at all. The computer wasn't this far to the left when I first came up here. And the angle is wrong. It was facing the attic's entrance, and now it's twisted around in the wrong direction. This is clear evidence that I was here, that I was up to something.

I can't leave without fixing it.

So I fall back into my crouch and push. As I heave the bulky monitor into position, it groans and screeches across the wooden floor. Uncle Phil's voice roars to life in my head, spewing the words he uses to avoid cussing in front of me.

Shiitake mushrooms. Fiddlesticks.

Finally, the computer is settled. I'm still amazed by its size and weight. I can't imagine using this ancient thing, and it's almost impossible to picture it in our office down the hall. The computer we have now is sleek and bright, its keys slender and whispery.

This one is its opposite. Boxy and bulky, with a wide, chunky keyboard.

With my heart hammering wildly in my chest, I scoop up the other Edith's box and scrabble down the ladder. Shove the ladder, slamming the overhead door shut.

And I bolt for my bedroom. Kick that door shut, too.

Fudge.

That was way too loud. Everything was way too loud.

But at least I have the box now. I take it to my closet and hide it inside my cedar art chest. I grab a pile of blankets and toss them over the closed trunk.

Then I sneak out of there and tiptoe back to the living room couch.

"Enjoy the bacon while you can," Mom says as she slides a few more greasy strips onto my plate. "I think it might be on the list."

We're seated around the table for breakfast. Our plates are filled with golden-brown waffles, sunny-side up eggs, and clusters of grapes. The white cotton curtains are shielding us from the early sunlight. Toast pops up in the toaster. Dad twists the cap off a bottle of orange juice.

"Are you ready for tomorrow?" Mom asks.

I reach across the counter to grab my toast. "What's tomorrow?"

"Your appointment with Dr. Ashworth."

The toast drops to my plate. Mom leans back in her seat. Dad clears his throat as he pours orange juice into three separate glasses.

"Did you forget?" she asks in her gentlest voice.

"No. I don't know."

I touch my fingertips to my two front teeth. The small gap in between.

Dad passes me the fullest glass. "Are you nervous about the procedure?"

"Not really." *Should I be?*

"It's okay if you are. We know it won't be easy for you." He reaches across the table, brushes my knuckles with his thumb. "But it won't last forever. We can go over the list and the schedule again, if you like. So that you'll know to expect."

I pull my hand away. "That's okay. I'm fine."

My parents exchange a quick, confused look. Then Dad starts slathering his toast in butter, while Mom takes a long sip of her orange juice.

"So." He lifts his voice, forcing optimism. "How's the short film coming along?"

"It's going."

"Did Serenity and Amelia like your drawings of the dog?" he asks.

I shrug. "Mostly."

"Mostly?" The orange juice hits the table with a smack. "What's that supposed to mean?"

I shrug a second time. Grab my toast, dip it into the bright yellow yolk. The egg's center bursts and spills all over my plate.

"How could they not *love* the little fellow?" Mom croons. "He's such a great muse for the film project."

"You didn't love him, either."

Her eyes widen with shock. "What?"

"The real dog," I remind her. "At the reservation. You told me to get away from him."

I shove the dripping toast into my mouth. Mom and Dad exchange looks again. This time, their expressions are full of silent alarm.

"That was different, sweetie," Dad says. "That was a real animal. A wild, *feral* animal."

I take my time to chew and swallow. "It was only a dog. A sweet little dog."

"He was a gigantic dog," Mom argues. "He might have hurt you."

"But he didn't."

"We don't know where he came from."

"But we could have found out. We could have helped him."

Mom flinches. Looks away from me. Lifts her hands to massage her temples. "There's nothing we could have done," she says. She unleashes a long sigh and adds, "I'm sorry."

"You're wrong," I tell her. "You're both wrong.

We could have done *something*. We could have helped him find his way home."

Dad says, "That's our point, sweetheart. He didn't have a home."

"Then we could have given him one." I rise from my chair. Carry my plate to the sink. "Thanks for breakfast, but I'm not that hungry."

My parents say nothing as I walk down the hall and shut myself inside my room.

9.

FLIP

July 6

The closet door glides open, and I lower myself to my knees. Push the blankets aside. Run my hand across the cedar chest's smooth, polished surface.

Unlatch its hinge.

The top creaks as I pull the lid up.

The other Edith's box looks wilted and old, with its worn cardboard and frayed edges. I lift it out, set it on the floor beside me.

Where are you from?

Amelia wants to go through this with me. And I promised I'll wait, but the anticipation is killing me.

Maybe if I peek at the pictures we've already seen, it won't count. My best friend said she wanted to *learn* everything about her. If I look in the box one more time, with a specific goal to learn nothing new, then how could she be mad? What could go wrong?

I lift the flaps. Reach for her head shot—the one with her faraway gaze.

If I were any good at drawing people, I would want to draw her. I would want to draw *this*. I wonder what she was looking at, what she was thinking about. I wonder when and where this photograph was taken.

I grab my nearest sketchbook and settle against the wall. Flip to a blank page and place it in my lap. Press my pencil to the center of the page.

A beat passes. Then I sketch a long, curved arc, followed by a second line in the same smooth motion. I draw a series of tiny lines between to connect them, all the way up the trunk. I pull my phone from my pocket and search for palm tree images to guide me as I draw its leafy head.

For the next hour, I sit and fill this sheet with palm trees along an imaginary shoreline. This sums up almost everything I know about Southern

California: palm trees and sunshine and beaches. Hollywood and glamorous people and hazy sunsets. I also know they have numerous sports teams and amusement parks. But that's it—nothing else.

And I know even less about the other Edith's heritage. Her culture. Her people. Did she grow up in Los Angeles, or was she born somewhere else? Was she raised on a reservation? Did she know recipes for fry bread?

My phone vibrates with a new text from Serenity.

Serenity: hey. how is everything? haven't heard from u today.

Me: I'm okay. How's your dad? How long will you be at his house? I brought the box down from the attic today. It's hidden in my room, so we can go through it later.

Serenity: soooo i guess u haven't brought it up with your parents? still sneaking around? and he is good. we're going camping later this week.

Me: No. Not going to bring it up with them. I asked where my name came from and they both lied to my face.

Serenity: *gasp* :O

Me: Yeah. We need to figure this out on our own.

When can you come over to help me go through the box?

Serenity: might have time tmrw. dad has the day off, he could drive me.

Me: Okay. Let me know if the afternoon will work. I have an appointment.

Serenity: what kind of appt?

Me: Tomorrow's the day I'm getting braces.

I sigh and set my phone aside. Stare at the drawing in my lap. The trees have slight bends in their trunks, careful angles of their palm leaves. I gave them different heights to make it more realistic, just as I do whenever I draw the mountains.

And yet, this landscape feels incomplete. But I'm not sure what to add to it. I don't know what else is missing.

10.

THE GAP

July 7

Before the summer began, I was looking forward to getting my braces. I was excited to get my teeth "fixed." But now that I'm here in the orthodontist's office, the thrill is gone. Completely.

I wait in the lobby as Mom fills out paperwork at the receptionist's desk. I can hear her pen against the clipboard, checking boxes, scribbling her signature.

There's an aquarium next to me, water glugging noisily through its filter. Bright blue rocks are layered over the bottom of the tank, with fake

plants sprouting through them, coral reef orna-
ments scattered at random. Several goldfish hover
near the glass walls, flat marble eyes flicking in
their sockets.

The other side of the room is designated for
kids. There's a crate filled with board puzzles. A
small table covered in activity sheets and crayons.
A bead roller coaster on the carpeted floor. A toddler is playing with it, knocking beads together,
chasing them along the loops and waves of colorful
wires. His mother is seated in a cushioned chair
nearby, with her young daughter balanced on her
knee. She's holding a copy of Dr. Seuss's book *Oh,
the Places You'll Go!* propped open in the girl's lap.
The mother's voice is soft as she recites the rhym-
ing lines.

The door to the patient rooms clicks open. A
woman in maroon scrubs peeks out into the lobby.
"Edie Green?"

Mom whirls around to look at me. "Ready?"

I nod and rise to my feet.

The woman grins. Her hair is pulled back in a
sleek, blonde ponytail. "Hi, there!" she says. "I'm
Kylie. It's so nice to meet you."

I return the smile, just to be polite.

"Wow," Kylie croons. "What a *beautiful* girl you are. So much like your momma. You guys must have some *great* genes in the family."

Mom smiles, but I can tell she feels awkward, just as I do. "That's sweet," she says. "Thank you." She steps forward, intercepting me in the middle of the lobby. Her fingertips brush against my forearm, and I stiffen under her touch. "Don't worry," she murmurs. "Everything will be fine. I promise."

I nod. Clench my jaw. And follow Kylie through the open door.

"Open up!"

I stare up at the U-shaped mold in Kylie's hands. I'm seated in a leather chair, in the center of a small room lined with white cabinets and glossy counters.

"Are you going to put me to sleep for the procedure?" I ask.

Kylie smiles. "No. The process of getting braces is painless."

I frown, skeptical. "I thought they'd make my mouth sore."

"Not right away, honey. You'll probably feel a little sore for a few days afterward, but not while you're here. Now," she says, gesturing with the mold, "open up."

I stretch my jaw, and Kylie leans in, positioning the mold over my bottom teeth.

"This is just for our records," she explains as she holds it in place. It's filled with a weird, pasty substance that oozes over my gums. "We're making an impression of your teeth."

She repeats the process, placing a mold over the top row. I can feel the press of the pasty substance as it hardens against my teeth. It almost reminds me of clay, or wet cement.

Kylie reclines my chair until I'm nearly horizontal. When she removes the molds, they make popping sounds, like suction cups.

"Excellent," she says. "Here, let me clean you up." She rinses and dabs around the inside of my mouth, removing the residue and remnants. "There. That's better. So tell me, what grade are you going into next year?"

"Seventh."

"Oh, fun," she chirps. "That's a good age. Enjoy it while it lasts; you won't ever be able to go back." She taps the corner of my mouth with a gloved finger. "Okay, open again. Thank you."

She spends the next few minutes cleaning my teeth, alternating between pulses of water and dashes of a minty polish.

"You really are so pretty," she says. "I love your hair color. It's such a rich, chocolaty brown. I think I might dye my hair soon. I'm sick of the blonde, I want to go dark. Like yours."

I hear the approach of footsteps, sneakers squeaking across the tiled floor.

"Dr. Ashworth," Kylie says. "We're almost done with the prep work. Our girl's just about ready for her braces."

"Great." Dr. Ashworth steps into view. Her blonde hair is streaked with gray, and tied back in a thick, cinnamon-roll-shaped bun. She's dressed in a white lab coat. The lower half of her face is concealed behind a white gauze mask. Her gray eyes are so deeply hooded, she almost looks sleepy. "Hello, Edie. It's so good to see you again."

I don't understand why they keep talking to me. It's not like I can respond, with the orthodontic tools stuck inside my mouth.

"Can you believe she's going to be a seventh grader soon?" Kylie chatters. "Growing up so fast!"

"I know," Dr. Ashworth says. She pulls my file

off the counter and starts flipping through its contents.

"And her smile will be so beautiful, with her teeth all nice and straight."

"Yes. A lovely smile for a lovely girl."

I can't help but cringe a little.

Kylie finishes the prep work. Dr. Ashworth sets my file aside, sits in a rolling chair, and wheels closer.

"Can I ask you a question?" The inside of my mouth feels chilly and clean as I speak.

Dr. Ashworth peers down at me. "Of course." Her voice is warm and honeyed, but her hooded gaze is purely clinical. Like I'm a frog she's about to dissect on a lab table.

I fidget in the chair. "What exactly is wrong with my gap tooth? I mean, will it cause any problems for me later on, or is this whole thing just—?" I don't want to say *pointless*, because it's her job to give people braces, and I don't want to hurt her feelings. But I can't think of any other alternatives.

"Cosmetic?" she supplies.

"Yeah." That works.

She tilts her head. "Gaps between teeth are typically a cosmetic issue," she admits. "Most people find that they're more confident and comfortable with their smiles once their gaps are fixed. But in your case, you also have a slight overbite. The top row of your teeth is protruding slightly over the bottom. It's mild, thankfully, so it isn't causing any real problems right now. But your braces will serve as a preventative treatment, to ensure your overbite won't become problematic. People with overbites are more susceptible to tooth decay, and they are at a considerably higher risk for developing gum disease. We wouldn't want either of those things to happen to you, Edie."

I must look uncomfortable, because Dr. Ashworth places a gentle hand on my shoulder. "I understand if you're a little scared. It's perfectly normal to get cold feet before the procedure. But I promise, the results will be worth it. You're a big girl. You'll do just fine with braces."

Dr. Ashworth secures a mouth prop over me, a hard rubber tool that disables me from closing my mouth. My tongue goes instantly dry. My throat feels a little itchy, and my eyes start to water.

Then she plants the first brackets around my back molars, metal rings that hug my teeth and bite into my gums. Kylie hands her the tools she needs and shines a UV light around in my mouth as Dr. Ashworth works from the back to the front.

I stare at the ceiling as the procedure carries on. I'm wearing shorts, and my exposed skin is starting to sweat against the leather seat, all clammy and sticky. The inside of my mouth feels cold and dry and full. My cheeks are sore and pinched.

Dr. Ashworth reaches my two front teeth. I try not to flinch as she presses the brackets against them.

When these braces come off, will I still look like the other Edith? Or will my smile be completely different? Will *I* be completely different?

My eyes water as she tightens the wire.

11.

DO THEY HURT?

July 7

"How do you feel?" Mom asks me.

I press my hand over my closed mouth. It feels like my lips are sticking way out. "Strange," I answer. "It feels unnatural."

Mom holds the glass door open for me as we exit the office building. The stone pathway leading back to the parking lot is dappled in shade and spots of sunlight.

"Do they hurt?"

"No."

"Good. They might be painful tomorrow, and

for a few days after. But at least they aren't hurting you yet."

When we reach the car, I buckle my seat belt and check my phone for missed messages.

Amelia: What are you doing right now?

Serenity: lmk when you're done getting braces! dad and i are in the north end. he said we can hang out for a little bit.

Rather than sending individual texts, I go back to our group chat and type my response there: Done getting braces. Come over in 20 mins.

I remove the other Edith's box from my art chest and place it on the floor between us.

"Has she responded yet?" I ask.

Serenity is hanging upside down over the edge of my bed with her feet propped up against the wall. She reaches for her cell phone, checks the screen. "Nope. Nothing."

I sigh. Glance out the window. Force my fingers through my hair, detangling the long strands.

Serenity arrived at my house nineteen minutes after I sent that text. Meanwhile, Amelia hasn't said anything. At all. Serenity and I have been waiting for over an hour.

What is up with her?

Serenity rolls over onto her stomach. "Are you really sure about this?"

"Sure about what?"

"Reading this stuff in private," she says. "Instead of just asking your parents about her."

"I already told you, they lied when I asked about my name. They'll probably deny the rest of it, too."

"I don't know. They might surprise you."

"They lied. They won't tell me anything."

"I doubt that."

Serenity bites her lip. "I can see why," she says. "But you shouldn't give up hope." She shifts again, sitting upright. "My parents kept the divorce a secret. For a really long time. I knew it was happening, and I thought for sure my dad would just . . . *leave*. In the middle of the night. I thought he'd sneak out and I'd never see him again. I used to go into his room and check the suitcase under his bed, to make sure he wasn't packed yet."

My fingers stop moving. I blink at Serenity.

I didn't know she did that. I didn't know she'd been afraid of him leaving.

"I know, I know," she says with a sigh. "Obviously, he didn't do it. He's better than that. And when my parents finally told me about the divorce, and explained how our lives would be from then on, I felt stupid for even thinking he'd leave me. But it made sense in my head, when I knew they were hiding something so big from me."

I look away. Swallow the rising lump in my throat.

"Parents can be weird," Serenity says. "That's for sure. They keep secrets. They don't always do the right thing. They make mistakes. But they're not *trying* to hurt you, Edie. If they lied, or they didn't tell you everything yet—there's a reason for it. And I think you should ask them about it, before we jump to our own conclusions."

"I didn't know you were afraid of your dad leaving," I tell her. "I didn't even know you knew about the divorce, before it happened. Why didn't you say anything?"

She shrugs. "Talking about it made it seem more real. And I didn't want to believe it was really happening." She draws a short breath. Drops her gaze to her hands. "I didn't want them to break up."

Silence fills the space between us. It grows and deepens.

Then a loud knock against my bedroom window jolts us both.

"Let me in!" Amelia shouts from the other side of the glass. "Don't start without me!"

I jump to my feet. Hold up one finger, to show her I'll be at the front door in a minute.

Serenity huffs and throws a pillow at the wall. "Would it *kill her* to answer her phone?"

I'm out the door and down the hall. I pull the front door open for Amelia, and she waltzes in with a casual "What have I missed?"

"Nothing. What took you so long?"

She shrugs. "Just busy. Nice braces, how do they feel?"

"They're okay. Busy doing what?"

"None of your beeswax," she says playfully. "And does it matter? I'm here now."

It matters. Lately, we've been so back and forth. One moment, she's stepping in to help me when I'm panicking in the attic. The next, she forgets to respond to my texts. She'll say that she likes my drawings, but she'll roll her eyes because my ideas for our film are "too cliché." She'll insist on going through the box with me, but then she shows up late and gives me a sassy nonresponse to explain herself. I keep noticing all these little moments, and they're adding up.

I want to be sure everything's okay between us.

Amelia starts to cross the room. "Come on," she says. "We'll go through the box. Then you need to hear my *brilliant* idea."

"Millie?"

She stops short. Her shoulder blades tighten beneath her shirt. This is a nickname I haven't used in a long time, since the first day of fifth grade. When our new teacher called roll and asked for our preferred nicknames, Amelia didn't correct him. He even clarified, *Don't you go by Millie? I met your parents on orientation night.* And she shook her head over and over. *Amelia is fine.*

When I called her Millie during lunch, she sighed and said she was done with nicknames. *We're fifth graders now*, she said. *Almost teenagers. Millie sounds like a little girl, but Amelia doesn't. That's why I need to start using it.*

And I remembered that request. From then on, she's been Amelia to me.

But right now, I think I need to remind her how long we've known each other. How important our friendship is.

I draw my breath. "Are we okay?"

She doesn't turn around. "Everything is fine, Edie. Can we go into your room and get started, please?"

I swallow. Push my suspicions and hurt feelings aside.

"Yeah," I say. "Let's go."

12.

THE BOX

July 7

"Do we have a plan here?" Serenity asks. "Like, where do we even start?"

Amelia says, "First, let's see if we can find her full name anywhere. Second, we'll look for the earliest thing we can find. It looks like she included dates on everything she wrote."

The three of us are gathered around the open box. We're in the middle of my bedroom, cross-legged on the floor.

Serenity glances at me. "Does that sound good to you, Edie?"

I nod. "Sure."

And so, we start going through the other Edith's stuff. Her private journals are pried apart. Her handwritten letters are freed from torn envelopes. Her head shots and postcards are flipped over, inspected.

I reach for a notebook with a thick black cover. Its edges are worn. Its middle is swollen. As I peel the cover open, an avalanche slides out: newspaper clippings. Loose flyers. Napkins scrawled with notes. Ticket stubs from the movie theater. A faded marigold-colored bus pass.

I squint at the text on the bus pass. The ink is barely visible, and the words are wrinkled. But I can still make out the route information.

"She was from here," I say. "Originally. She took a one-way bus from Seattle to Los Angeles."

"Of course she did," Amelia says excitedly. "She left to pursue her dream career!"

I nod my agreement. Scan the ticket. "This is dated October 1973."

"Good work, Edie. I'll see if I can find anything from before that."

As Amelia surges ahead, I feel a sudden twinge of . . . something in my stomach. Guilt? Discomfort?

I guess the reality of what we're doing just hit me. We're going through the other Edith's private belongings. Ripping through journals that might've contained her thoughts and secrets. Reading through letters that probably contained personal conversations.

Maybe we have no business doing this. Maybe this box should go back in the attic.

"I don't think she was technically from Seattle," Serenity says.

Amelia scrunches her nose. "What makes you say that?"

"Look at the envelopes." Serenity holds one up in demonstration. "Her letters were all sent to the same address in Indianola, Washington. The post-cards, too."

They both look at me. I can't help but shrink under their gazes.

Amelia asks, "Do you know anyone who lives in Indianola?"

"No." I shake my head for emphasis. "I've never even *heard* of Indianola."

"You're sure? You've never been there?"

"Definitely not."

Do my parents know where Indianola is? Have

they been there before?

I sit in stunned silence as my friends continue to pick through this stuff. My chest feels clogged as I watch them unfold her letters, skim their fingers down the pages of loopy cursive. Amelia discards one of the head shot photos with a careless flick. Serenity squints at an official-looking document.

"Whoa," she says. "Look at this report from her doctor's appointment. It has her height and weight and everything. The last four digits of her social security number. Her date of birth." Serenity glances my way. "Her full name."

I go rigid. A bolt of ice pierces my gut.

"What is it?" Amelia demands. She clambers forward, scooting to look over Serenity's shoulder.

I'm frozen, still processing the meaning of her words. *It has her height and weight and everything. The last four digits of her social security number.*

It's too much. Too much information about a total stranger.

"Edith Anne Graham," Amelia announces, loud and triumphant. "Google it. Let's see if she was famous."

"Keep your voice down," I shout-whisper, but she ignores me. Her phone is already out, fingertips flying as she types.

All three of us hold our breath as we wait.

Then Amelia's shoulders deflate. "No," she says. "Zero results. It doesn't look like she was anyone important."

Her words make me flinch. I drop my gaze to my hands.

This was a bad idea. I shouldn't have brought the box down here. We shouldn't be doing this.

I'm about to say so, but Amelia manages to cut me off.

"Look at this, though," she says excitedly. "I found a journal entry from September 1973. One month before the bus ticket."

And the curiosity wins out.

Amelia pulls the open journal into her lap and skims for a moment. Then she reads aloud: "Today," she says, "my life takes on a new course and a new meaning. I've decided to take a chance and pursue my dreams.

"Earlier this year, Sacheen Littlefeather inspired me. She was the young woman who rejected an Academy Award on behalf of Marlon Brando. I'm still awed by the amount of courage it must have taken, to approach the stage with her head held high, to stand and speak before that booing audience. She was graceful and brave, and beautiful in her—" Amelia pauses, struggling with the next word. "*Regalia?* And it was terribly clever to use that platform to draw attention to Wounded Knee. The media has been mostly silent on the events unfolding there, until now. Thanks to Sacheen Littlefeather and her ally, these issues can no longer be ignored.

"Theo went to South Dakota in the spring. He joined the Oglala Lakota in solidarity with their cause. Theo has always been greatly involved in activist efforts. I wanted to join him when he protested at our own Fort Lawton a few years back, but Theo is fiercely protective of me. When everything escalated, he insisted that I stay home. And perhaps it was for the best, since so many activists were arrested. Including my big brother.

"But regardless of the risks, some part of me still wished to be there. I want to do brave, productive things in my life. Like the activists at Fort Lawton and Wounded Knee. Like Theo and Sacheen. I'm twenty-one years old now, and it's time for me to stop living within my own little bubble. I love my home, I love my family, and I don't mind my part-time job at the ferry docks. But there are bigger things I could be doing. Or at the very least, there are things I could *try* to accomplish.

"Which is why I've purchased a bus ticket for California. I'm going to Los Angeles to pursue a career in the film industry. I've always wanted to be an actress, ever since I was a little girl. No matter how unrealistic or idealistic the dream might be, I've secretly clung to it with my whole heart. I believe that Sacheen Littlefeather's speech will open doors for us. Doors that have been shut too tight, for far too long."

Amelia flips the page. Lifts her head. "That's the whole entry."

I blink at her. "I feel like I only understood about half of what she talked about." I glance between my two friends. "Who's Sacheen Littlefeather? And what are the Og—what was that term? Og-something? The protestors she talked about."

She flips back to the previous page. "Oglala Lakota."

"Right. What does that mean?"

"They're a Native American tribe," Serenity says. She has her phone in her hand, a web browser opened on the screen. "A part of the Sioux

Nation. And Sacheen Littlefeather is a Native American activist."

Serenity meets my gaze. Amelia glances my way, too.

My stomach rumbles, giving me an excuse to put everything away. "I'm hungry," I say. "Let's finish this later." I reach for the scattered papers and scoop them all up, placing them back inside the box. "Do either of you want sandwiches? Or maybe Mom will order us a pizza?"

"No, thanks." Amelia shifts onto her knees. "Don't you want to hear my idea?"

"Okay. What is it?"

"Well, I was *thinking*—maybe the other Edith could be our inspiration for the film? We can reenact parts of her life, and cast you as the lead, since you look so much like her! Then our film would be 'based on true events,' which would make our mini movie super popular. People love stuff like that." She shoots me a toothy grin. "What do you think? Am I a genius or what?"

An awkward silence. I open my mouth, but nothing comes out other than "Oh."

"It would've been better if it turned out you were secretly related to someone famous. If that were the case, we'd probably get attention from news outlets, maybe even real reporters from Hollywood. But still, I think this could work, whether or not she was in any movies."

"But—" I blink several times, staring at her. "But I can't. Public speaking is one of my biggest fears." My voice dwindles to a whisper. "That's why I'm the animator. So I don't have to be on camera."

We've already decided. We've discussed this so many times.

"I know," Amelia says stubbornly. "But how often does stuff like *this* happen? Why would we want to come up with our own story when we could use something real? Something interesting and cool and different." She gestures at the box. "We've read *one* journal entry. We have a lot left to learn about her, but this girl left everything behind to pursue her dreams in LA. Don't you want people to know about her? Don't you want her legacy to carry on, somehow?"

Serenity shifts beside me. "I don't know about this."

Amelia reaches for my hands, gives them a squeeze. "Think it over," she urges. "Please."

And I promise her I will, because really, what else could I say?

13.

UNCLE PHIL'S BIRTHDAY PARTY

July 9

I hate my braces. I actually *hate* them.

My teeth are so sore, I can feel their aching roots deep in my jaw. And I didn't know it was possible for the tips of your teeth to feel sensitive, tender to the touch. But oh, it is. It hurts to chew. It hurts to brush my teeth. It hurts to smile.

And everyone keeps telling me to smile.

Including Uncle Phil.

"Hoo boy." He gives a low whistle. "That's a lot of metal in there, kid! The gap already looks a little smaller. Must be one he—I mean, one *heck* of an orthodontist you've got."

My parents and I have just arrived at his house, for his birthday party. Uncle Phil's blond hair is mussed, and his blue eyes are bright with mischief. His cheeks are reddish, and his nose is sunburned and flaking.

"Do they hurt, kiddo?"

I shrug, because he might tease me if I say yes. He used to poke fun at me all the time. Not because he's mean or anything; that's just his sense of humor. When I was little, he used to pinch my nose and pretend to pull it off my face. Then he'd poke his thumb out of his closed fist and say, "I've got your nose!" He never actually tricked me, but he thought my straight-faced reactions were hilarious.

Uncle Phil grins, approving. "Tough girl."

He leads us through his house, into the backyard. Hamburger patties are sizzling on the open grill. The sun-bleached patio bakes beneath my sandals. A funny little garden gnome stands guard by Uncle Phil's squash patch. And he has a kiddie pool set up for his pet duck, William. He's the only person I know who has a pet duck, and it's one of my favorite things about him. Two men linger on the patio, holding brown glass bottles in their hands.

"Chuck, Bran—this is my sister, Lisa, and her husband, Donnie." He claps my shoulder. "And my all-time favorite niece, Edie."

Chuck and Bran greet us with nods and hellos.

"I hope you guys are ready for some burgers," Uncle Phil says as he steps in front of the grill. "We're feastin' like royalty tonight."

We eat dinner inside.

The adults spend at least twenty minutes talking about traffic. *Traffic.* Uncle Phil and his friends go on these huge rants about their daily commutes, and the construction on a local bridge that has been clogging up the freeway, and Mom and Dad chime in with their own stories about driving around the area. Then their conversation switches to *taxes.* Which is confusing and dull. Even though they all have strong opinions about "their tax dollars." *Our tax dollars should be going to this, not that. Our tax dollars shouldn't do this particular thing at all. Our tax dollars are clearly out of control. Our tax dollars are blah blah blah.*

I've never been so bored in my life.

And I'm losing patience with my parents.

I've given them so many opportunities to come

forward with the truth. I keep dropping hints and hoping for answers about Edith Graham. Amelia, Serenity, and I didn't learn much more, beyond that first journal entry. Serenity's dad came to pick her up after our late lunch, and Amelia left around the same time she did.

So I put the box away and took my drawing pad out to the backyard, where Mom was gardening. I pretended to work on sketching stuff while I asked her seemingly random questions, like: *Hey, Mom, have you ever been to Los Angeles? Do you know anyone who lived there?*

And instead of telling the truth, she played dumb again.

I don't understand why the other Edith is such a big secret.

"So how long will the kid need braces?" Uncle Phil asks.

Dad shrugs. "Dr. Ashworth doesn't know for sure yet, but she'll probably need them for at least nine months."

Uncle Phil whistles. "Long time. And there are all kinds of foods she can't eat while she's got those contraptions, right?"

Dad nods. "It's a pretty big list. She's not allowed

to have popcorn, caramel, anything that contains nuts, chips, pretzels—"

Uncle Phil looks horrified. "You're kidding me. You just described my whole diet, especially when I was a *kid*. Poor girl."

I nibble carefully around the edges of a triangular watermelon slice. The fruit is dark pink and freckled with little white seeds. Its juice leaks out the corner of my mouth and dribbles down to my chin. Then, without thinking, I grab my napkin, press it against my jawline, and cringe in pain.

"*Ugh.*" I drop the napkin and the watermelon slice.

Mom's hand appears on my shoulder. "Are you okay, Edie?"

I shrug her off. "I'm fine."

"Are your braces hurting?"

"They're fine. Little chunks of food keep getting stuck between the wires and brackets. But it's okay."

She still looks overly concerned. "If they're bothering you too much, we could get you something else for dinner. Maybe you could just have a smoothie? Phil, do you have a blender?"

I open my mouth to protest, but Uncle Phil is

already on his feet. "Sure thing," he says. "I've got some bananas, some strawberries. What would the kid like?"

My teeth grind painfully together. I try to respond, but once again, I'm rudely interrupted.

"Do you have any greens? Spinach or kale, maybe?" Dad asks. "I don't want her iron levels to get too low."

"Donnie. No offense, man, but I never have that stuff in my fridge. I'm very anti-kale."

"Really?" Dad sounds shocked. "But it's a super-food."

"Whatever you have is fine, Phil. I'm just worried about the pain—" Mom reaches out to tuck a strand of hair behind my ear, and I shove her hand away.

"I *said* I'm *fine.*"

Silence swoops down over the room like a bird of prey. Everyone stops talking and moving. Silverware stills against plates. Burgers freeze halfway to mouths. All eyes are on me.

I want to disappear.

My cheeks burn hot with guilt.

I didn't mean to push my mother's hand like that. But she's not listening to me. No one around this table is. If they'd just let me speak, then they'd know that I don't want anything. I don't need anyone fussing over me.

I break the spell by scooting away from the table, staggering out of my chair. "I'm going outside for a minute," I mutter. "Want some fresh air."

I catch a glimpse of Uncle Phil's stunned face before I turn and leave for the backyard.

I burst through the sliding door and slam it shut with a glass-rattling slap. I walk over to the edge of the patio. Drop down onto my butt. Hug my knees to my chest.

I'm just so sick of this. Of not knowing anything. Of them still treating me like a little kid.

The sliding door eases open and shut behind me, followed by Uncle Phil's footsteps.

He sits down beside me. He doesn't say anything.

William is splashing around in his little kiddie pool. He swims in circles, dunking his emerald-green head underwater, flinging water droplets as he shakes his beak.

The silence stretches between us, like the rolling weight of the summer heat. The concrete patio bakes my skin through my denim shorts. The sun warms my back, my dark hair. I can feel beads of sweat gathering across my forehead, against my neck, all along my hairline.

William turns and starts quacking. And quacking. And *quacking*. He quacks and honks and flaps his little wings, all while staring at Uncle Phil.

Eventually, Uncle Phil sighs. And then, in the most serious voice I've ever heard him use, he looks at William and says, "What the duck do you want?"

It's probably the dumbest joke in history. But I can't help it. I snort so loud, I have to clap my hands over my mouth. Another shock of pain hits my teeth, but it doesn't stop the rush of giggles as they erupt out of me.

Uncle Phil side-eyes me. "There she is," he says. "There's my niece." He reaches over and musses up my hair. I bat his hand away, and he lets it fall back to his side.

William finally stops quacking and resumes his diving routine. He's showing off for us, fanning and ruffling his tail feathers.

"So," Uncle Phil says. "You wanna explain what happened in there? It's not like you to be so snappy."

I hug my knees tighter against my chest.

"Did I do something that upset you?" he asks.

He ducks his head in an attempt to meet my gaze. "You can tell me."

I scratch my elbow. Avoid his gaze. "Not really."

"Edie," he says. "If something's bothering you—I'd really appreciate it if you told me. Especially if there's anything I can do to help."

I consider his words. Peek up at him. "Uncle Phil," I say. "Can I ask you about something that happened a long time ago?"

"Of course."

"You can't tell my mom, though."

"I'm her big brother. It's my job to keep secrets from her."

"You can't tell my dad, either."

He shrugs. "Okay."

My phone is a heavy lump in my pocket. As I trace it with my fingertips, I think of Serenity's advice to confront my parents. I remember Amelia's insistence that we keep the box a secret. And I decide that discussing this stuff with Uncle Phil is probably harmless.

So I ask him, "Do you know where my name came from?"

He hides his reaction well, but I still catch it. The slight widening of his pupils.

"Your name?"

"Yes. Edith."

"Are you asking because you're curious, or . . . because you think you know where it came from?"

"A little bit of both."

I explain the discovery of the box. Without even meaning to, I tell him everything that's happened over the past few days. I tell him about my friends' reactions. I tell him about how my parents keep evading my questions. I tell him about the journal entry we read. I tell him about Amelia's new idea for the film, which I promised to consider, even though I'm not comfortable with it at all.

"I just want to know who she was. I want to know why I was named after her, and I don't understand why they've never *told* me about her. It makes no sense."

Uncle Phil stares at me. As I catch my breath after my long rant, I stare back at him. His blue eyes are unexpectedly sad.

A thought pops up in my head. "Do you know anything about her?" I ask. "Do you know who the other Edith was?"

His throat bobs as he swallows. He looks away, but I can't stop examining his face. The heavy lines around his mouth and under his eyes. The creases drawn along his forehead. The gray in his stubble.

Uncle Phil looks . . . older, all of a sudden.

"I can't lie to you, Edie." He sighs. "Never been able to. And I'm not about to start now."

The fine hairs along my arms stand up. My fingers knot together in my lap.

And then he says, "I know where your name came from, kiddo. I know who Edith Graham was." His eyes squeeze shut. "But I'm sorry; I can't tell you anything about her."

14.

UNDER ATTACK

July 9

No.

My heart hiccups in my chest. I blink once, hard. This was not the answer I'd expected.

"Oh. Why not?"

"I'm sorry." Uncle Phil can't even look at me. "But it shouldn't be me. It has to be your mother. Your friend Serenity is right. You should go to her yourself. Ask about Edith Graham."

I shake my head over and over. "I can't. I promised Amelia I'd go through the box with her and—"

"I know you did, love. You're a good friend for

wanting to keep your promises. But this situation is . . . unique. And if she's as good a friend as you are, she'd let you discuss it with your parents. She'd care more about you knowing your own truth, instead of focusing on her ideas for the film."

My response is automatic: "She *is* a good friend. She's one of my best friends."

He glances at me now. His expression is skeptical and I hate it.

"But that's not the point right now," I say. "I want you to tell me about the other Edith."

"I can't."

"Yes, you can."

"It can't be me," he insists softly. "It has to be your mother. You'll understand when you learn the truth. She always planned on telling you about her, Edie. She didn't want to keep it a secret forever."

My jaw drops. *"What?"*

He gives a single nod. "It's true. She was just waiting until you were old enough."

"How old is old enough? Why do I need to be a certain age?"

He scrubs his face with both hands. "You'll see, Edie. I'm sorry I can't say more."

Nothing makes sense to me anymore. Shouldn't

I be the first to know about the woman I was named after? Why are they making it such a big deal?

"Please try to trust your parents. Edie. They're only doing what they believe is best."

"That doesn't make it right."

"Maybe not. But their goal was never to lie to you. They just wanted to protect you."

"Lying to someone is a weird way to protect them."

"Touché." He smiles. Musses my hair. "There's something else I can tell you. A story from our family's history."

I lift my gaze. "What is it?"

He draws a quick breath. "So," he says. "I was a deckhand on a commercial fishing boat for many years. I was mainly stationed out at Bristol Bay, for months at a time. Through stormy seas and cold, clear days. Waking up as early as three or four in the morning. It was a tough and dangerous life, but I made good money, and I didn't see any real reason to stop.

"The year you were born, we had our biggest salmon run in years. We couldn't reel the fish in fast enough. We broke records. We made tons of money. I came home and bought you all kinds of clothes and toys, because I loved spoiling my baby niece. I spent a lot of time with your parents. It was too bad my own parents were gone before you came along, but having you made it easier for me to cope with that loss. That first year of your life was one of the best in mine.

"It was hard, going back to the boat after I met you. And that following season, the one right after our biggest haul, was . . . well, it was terrible. There were almost no fish left in those waters." He swallows. His voice drops. "It was our own fault; we took too many hauls the previous year. Not enough salmon were able to return to their spawning beds. We threw the whole ecosystem off-balance. The longer I stayed, the emptier those nets became, the more I realized that I was in the wrong business. I was a part of something destructive. And I wanted out. So I left."

"Just like that?"

"Just like that. I've been involved in ecological restoration projects ever since. I also work with a lot of local tribes who are trying to save their traditional fishing rights." He pauses. Glances at me. "I know this story probably seems very random, Edie. But believe me, it's loosely related to Edith

Graham. To everything that happened between her and your mother. And their tribal nation, their sovereignty. It's all connected."

"Okay," I say. Even though I trust his word, I'm not sure what else to say. It feels like he just gave me a riddle to solve.

"I want you to trust me," he says. "And talk with your parents. No more hiding, no more secrets." He claps his hands and rubs them together. "In the meantime, here's a question for you: Do you think you'll be able to eat some birthday cake? Or are your teeth too sore?"

"You know, I'm not a little kid anymore. You can't just say something about desserts and expect me to forget everything and move on."

He throws his head back and laughs. "Kiddo! That was not my intention at all. Even though it was *extremely* effective when you were small."

"Can't you at least tell me *one* thing about her?"

"Absolutely not."

I widen my eyes and pout, giving him my best impression of a puppy dog.

Uncle Phil shields his face with his arm. "No," he says sternly. "No way. Not falling for that."

I press forward, craning to get back in his line of sight.

"Cut that out. Stop it. *Enough*." In the background, William sits upright in the water and quacks. "I'm talking to you, too, duck!"

A giggle rises in my throat. "Be nice to William."

Uncle Phil scoffs. "William should be nice to *me*. I'm the one under attack here."

In a swift motion, Uncle Phil grabs me around the waist and starts tickling me. I kick and scream and roar with laughter, but he holds tight, refusing to let go.

"This is what happens!" His voice rumbles against me. "This is what you get when you side with the duck!"

I'm laughing so hard, tears are forming in the corners of my eyes. It's like we've gone through a time warp, and I'm tiny and helpless against his tickle attacks all over again.

When he releases me, I still can't stop giggling and gasping.

"Fine," I manage to say. "Let's go eat cake."

"That's my girl," Uncle Phil declares. "But one last thing, before we go back inside—you have my number in your phone, right?"

I resist the urge to roll my eyes. We don't text too regularly, but whenever we do, he ends his messages with "Thanks, Uncle Phil" or "Love, Phil."

As if I don't have his name and number entered into my contacts.

"Yes," I tell him. "Of course I do."

He nods. "Good. If you ever want to talk about this again after you have that conversation with your mother, or you want to discuss anything else—anything at all—just shoot me a text."

"I will. Thank you."

We both get to our feet.

"And you won't tell my parents we talked?"

"Not a chance. What are uncles for?"

As we approach the sliding door, Uncle Phil throws his arm around my shoulders. I lean into the hug, wrapping my arms around his belly.

15.

WHAT'S HER NAME?

July 9

"Haaappy birthday to you!"

A single candle is lit in the middle of a round chocolate cake. The frosting is thick and perfect and smooth. Uncle Phil blows out the candle, and we all clap and cheer.

"Well, that was fun. Thank you all." He rubs his hands together. "While Chuck serves up the cake, I'm gonna open Edie's present. Be sure to give the first slice to my niece. And give her plenty of ice cream, too. Nice and easy on the teeth." Uncle Phil glances around himself. "Now, what did my niece get for me this year?"

"Edie," Dad says. "Go get it for him, please."

I hurry off to grab the gift bag from the living room. The tissue paper crinkles as I carry it back to the table, placing it in front of Uncle Phil.

"Thanks, kiddo."

He pulls my gift closer and digs inside the bag for the card. His eyes pop as he pulls it free from the clouds of tissue paper.

"Holy smokes. Look at this." He turns the hand-made card around, showing everyone in the room.

I go pink. It's not *that* big of a deal. I just drew a picture of the dog and William, sitting together in a summer meadow. I included little lines around the dog's tail, to show he's wagging and happy. And William has a small bubble floating above his beak, filled with the word *Quack!*

"It looks like William made a friend," Uncle Phil says proudly. He taps the picture. "What's her name?"

"I think we're calling him Bruno," I tell him. "He's a boy."

"Edie and her friends are making a short film this summer," Dad says. "And this dog is her muse. She's working on the animation."

Uncle Phil's jaw drops. "She's doing *what* now?"

"I told you there was a film, Uncle Phil."

"Sure, you said you were making a short film with your friends, but you didn't say anything about drawing pictures for it."

"Oh. Well. I am." I sink in my chair a little bit, aware of everyone's eyes on me. "I wanted to try something I've never done before."

"That's amazing," Uncle Phil says. "Absolutely incredible. So—how does it work? Will all the images be this detailed? This colorful? Are you some kind of prodigy, destined to animate award-winning films for Disney?"

I shake my head. "Most of the drawings will be pretty basic. Pencil sketches that show outlines and movement. But I want the ending to become more colorful, so that the final image will be a full-color landscape, if that makes sense?" This was our idea, from the very beginning. I don't mention the fact that Amelia has been having second thoughts, because Uncle Phil already seems skeptical of her and I don't want to make her sound like a bad friend.

Mom nods. "They're entering a youth film festival this August. Her art teacher, Mrs. Barnes, tutored her in basic animation techniques, and Donnie installed the video editing software on our computer at home. He's going to help the girls out with that aspect."

"Unbelievable," he says. "My niece is a twelve-year-old genius."

I shy away from the praise. "You're exaggerating."

"I'm really not." He returns his attention to the card. "So this little dog is your main star, huh? Will William also make an appearance?"

"I don't know. I actually don't even know if we're going to keep the dog in the film. We haven't settled on a story yet."

"Keep the dog. Definitely keep the dog."

He sets the card aside and fishes his present out of the bag.

It's not much. Just a project I started in my after-school drawing club, which turned into a small canvas painting. The background is blue, and William is pictured in the center of it. I used a generic photograph of a mallard for reference, but Uncle Phil doesn't need to know that. I know that when he looks at it, he will only see William, and that's what matters most.

For a long moment, Uncle Phil doesn't say a word. He doesn't do anything at all.

And then he lifts his gaze. And his voice is low and clear as he says, "I love it, kiddo. Thank you."

Before he even bothers to try his slice of cake, Uncle Phil sets out on a mission to find the perfect spot in his house to display the painting. He settles on a blank spot above his fireplace, and he hangs it there, making the tiniest adjustments until the canvas is perfectly set against the wall.

Mom touches my shoulder and leans in to whisper, "So thoughtful, Edie."

A knot tightens in my chest. Uncle Phil's words echo in my head.

Please try to trust your parents, Edie. They're only doing what they believe is best.

His advice was so similar to Serenity's. They both want me to come clean, to tell my parents I found the box, to be honest with them about how I'm feeling.

But I just don't know if I can. My trust has been broken.

16.

THE METHOD

July 9

The moon is outside my window. Its face is full and round, skin blemished with craters, and white as milk. I can't believe how close it feels, how big its presence is. I feel like I could cast a fishing line out into the sky and reel it in, tugging as it bobs through the currents of stars.

I flop over in my bed. Kick until my legs are free from the tangled blankets.

Serenity must've lost service in the woods. Her last text to me was, **we've almost made it to our camping spot,** and that was three hours ago. I've texted her twice since then: UNCLE PHIL KNOWS ABOUT EDITH GRAHAM! and For some reason, he refused to tell me anything about her. He said it should all come from my mom. I really wonder why.

I sent the same messages to Amelia, who said that we should hang out and discuss it tomorrow. She said that she has plans to go to Pike Place Market with her mom and brother, and I should tag along, which is what I'll do.

Now I swing my legs over the edge of my bed, toes curling silently over the floorboards. I rise to my feet. My nightgown swishes around my calves. The closet door creaks as I push it open. I settle onto my knees and slide the box toward me across the floor. Silver moonlight spills through the window, illuminating the floorboards. The papers whisper against one another as I pick through them. I retrieve an envelope and tilt it toward the moonlight to read the delivery information.

The letter was addressed to a Mr. T. Graham, in Indianola, Washington.

It was written by a Miss E. Graham, from Los Angeles, California.

I release a hushed gasp. Brush my fingertips

across the penned letters.

I slip my fingers inside the envelope and pull out the letter. It's dated December 14, 1973. Ten days before Christmas Eve. I hold my phone up, beaming its flashlight across the page as I read:

December 14, 1973

Dear Theo,

I hope this message finds you well, big brother. I've heard you've had a terribly cold winter. How are you and Mom? How's everyone back home? I miss you all so much.

These first few months in Los Angeles have been so interesting. I'm still working as a waitress, as I mentioned in my previous phone call. And I've also been taking acting lessons. My teachers are all very knowledgeable about the Method. Method acting emphasizes the need to "become" the character. To embody their experiences. To view the world through their eyes.

They've also told me about the star system. Movie studios used to sign deals with actors and actresses, in exchange for creating their personas and controlling their lives. Sandy, a girl in my acting class, claims it was easier to get gigs back then. That all you had to do was get discovered, and the studio took care of everything: your name, your image, which films you starred in, even who you went on dates with.

I didn't say anything to Sandy, but in my opinion, the star system sounds dreadful. I would hate to let anyone control me that way. I much prefer the way things are now, even if it's harder to build a reputation on your own. I'd rather take these lessons, immerse myself in the Method, and let my own storytelling skills do the work for me.

I truly believe that what you put out into the world comes back. And I am pouring my whole heart into my work. It's possible that I won't land any leading roles, or even supporting roles, but I feel good being here. I'm enjoying my acting classes. I even like bussing tables in the restaurant, chatting with guests when I have a chance, and swapping stories with my coworkers. Regardless of whether or not I achieve what I came here for, I believe I'm doing something, just being here. Being me.

But I do have some news to share, big brother. An update that might become something, or could turn out to be nothing at all. I have an audition after the holidays. I'm trying out for a role in a major romantic comedy. The chances are slim to none, but that won't stop me from putting myself out there.

I'll be sure to tell you more, as I learn more myself. Let's talk on the phone again soon. I love you.

Love,
Edith

My heart is beating hard and fast. She had an audition? For a major romantic comedy?

I know I should wait for my friends. I know I promised Amelia we'd go through the whole box together, but I can't help it. I just want to find one more piece of information for the night. I want to see if she wrote about the audition again.

I'm skimming her letters from January 1974. Squinting at her cursive. It's really neat and pretty in some paragraphs, then it gets all slanted and jumbled in others. It seems like her handwriting got sloppy when she shared exciting news.

Which is why it takes me five tries to read the letter she wrote after the audition.

I gasp in the silence. My hands fly to my mouth.

Amelia's voice pops up in my head: *Zero results. It doesn't look like she was anyone important.*

She was wrong. *Google* was wrong. This letter changes everything.

17.

GIVE HER A CHANCE

July 10

I have Edith Graham's letter folded tight and tucked inside my deepest pocket. As I ride my bike to Amelia's house, I can feel the wad press against my leg each time the pedals rotate. I bump over cracks in the sidewalk before I pull into her driveway. It's still pretty early in the morning, and her front yard glistens with beads of dew.

I dash to the front door; she opens it within seconds.

"Hey. You said you had news about the other Edith?"

"Yes. Big news." I kick my shoes off beside the welcome mat, among the strappy sandals and brightly colored sneakers. "When are we leaving for Pike Place?"

"Mom and Adam are still getting ready. Let's go to my room to talk."

We hurry down the hall and up the stairs. I scuttle inside her room, and she snaps the door shut behind us.

"Okay," I say as I dig inside my pocket. "I found proof that she was in a movie. A huge Hollywood film."

Amelia's eyebrows shoot up. "Really? You have my *full* attention."

I explain the first hint I found last night, about the audition for a role in a romantic comedy. "She didn't get that part," I tell her. "But they liked her, and offered her a role in a different thing they were working on."

"Was she the lead actress?"

"I don't think so. But they gave her a few speaking lines." I open the letter and hold it up between us. Amelia steps close, and we read her words together:

January 7, 1974

Dear Theo,

I'm in! I wasn't accepted into the original picture I told you about. But the producers liked my audition, and they've given me a role in their upcoming Western! Now, I know what you're thinking. When I came here, I swore I wouldn't do any Westerns. But this one is going to be different. They showed me the script, and it is so progressive. It's called **When the West Was Theirs,** *and I can't wait to be a part of it. This will be my first time speaking on-screen!*

Call me as soon as you get this message. I'm dying to explain in greater detail.

All my love,
Edith

"Wow," Amelia says. "This is actually really cool. She must have been good, if they offered her a role in a different movie!"

"Totally!" I tell Amelia more about her previous letter, about her acting lessons and general determination.

"This is great stuff, Edie. Did you look up the movie she was in? *When the West Was Theirs?*"

I shake my head. Amelia whips her phone out and types the title into a web browser. She scrolls through the top hits: movie posters, critical reviews, a link to a trailer. She clicks on the preview and hits play.

An announcer's voice talks over the footage. He describes the plot without giving too many details. Action shots flash across the screen: cowboys on horseback, pistols gleaming at their hips; quiet villages of tepees; violent war scenes; a kiss between a cowboy and a Native girl.

Amelia suddenly shouts, "That was her!"

She pauses the video with her fingertip. Drags it backward. Hits play.

I watch closely.

It's another village scene, and the camera is angled to show several women seated around a bonfire. Sure enough, Edith Graham is among them. She's wearing a tan dress, long beaded necklaces, and moccasins. Her hair is styled in two braids and her gaze is distant. Like she's watching something happen from miles away.

"This is amazing," Amelia says proudly. "Good

work, Edie. We can definitely use all this new information in our film. We're going to have the best story in the entire festival."

I glance at her, eyebrows lifted. She smiles at me awkwardly.

"I mean, *if* we decide to go with her story. Which I really think we should."

Before I can react or say anything, the doorbell rings downstairs.

Amelia exits the video and stuffs the phone inside her pocket. She bites her bottom lip, the way she does whenever she feels guilty or anxious.

"Oh," she says. "By the way, I forgot to tell you. Another friend is going downtown with us."

"Did Serenity come back from her dad's house early?"

"No, not her. Someone else from our grade."

"Who?"

The doorbell rings again, long and drawn out, like someone is holding the button down.

"Edie," she says. "Please, don't judge. Just give her a chance."

Amelia throws her bedroom door open and pounds back down the stairs. I follow at the same pace, confused and a little hurt by her words. *Don't judge?* Why would I judge her for wanting to invite another friend? I skid to a stop at the bottom of the staircase, at the same moment the front door opens.

Libby.

Amelia's voice goes high and squeaky as she greets her. "Hi! I'm so glad you made it!" And now she's stepping aside, gesturing for Libby to come in.

My heart kicks violently inside my chest.

Libby comes in and removes her shoes on the doormat like she's supposed to. She doesn't even ask first, and it's as if she knows the rules in Amelia's house. As if she's been here before. Libby smiles and says, "Sorry I'm late." And Amelia is insisting it's okay, no worries at all, she's just *so glad* she's here. And I'm watching and listening, but I can't believe it. What *is* this? What's happening? Libby finally looks up and realizes I'm here. Our gazes lock and I can't move. Her grin turns smug, like a crocodile lurking in murky waters.

She nods once, and says, "Edie."

Amelia turns to me. Her smile is wide and forced. "Libby is coming downtown with us. We're all going to have so much fun."

Libby says, "I heard you got braces."

And I can't form words. I can't even breathe.

"Well," Libby says, baring her own teeth at me. "Can I see?"

I guess I don't have a choice. I open my mouth, pulling my lips back from the brackets.

Libby's eyes gleam, and her lips twist into another version of that creepy smile. "Nice," she says, in a falsely sweet voice. "That's good. You needed them."

Then Amelia's mom and brother come downstairs, and we're ushered out the door and into the car. The back seat is cramped with Adam in his booster seat, me in the middle, and Libby's giant legs sprawling into my space. I'm blinking and stunned, trying to catch Amelia's gaze in the rearview mirror, but she won't look my way. Her mother reverses out of the driveway.

I wasn't expecting this. I didn't see it coming.

18.
PULLING AWAY

July 10

Libby and I were almost friends, once. Before she started calling me "Granny." Before she had any problems with me.

She was the new girl in fourth grade. Our first seating chart was alphabetical, and Libby was behind me, because her last name is Gast. I remember our laminated nameplates—*Liberty G.* and *Edith G.*—printed in cursive fonts, with graphics of yellow pencils and shiny red apples. I remember asking her if she'd like to sit with me during lunch, since she didn't know anyone yet, and she smiled wide and accepted my offer.

So we sat together for lunch. And we hung out at recess. And she seemed to fit in well with Serenity and Amelia, and everything was going great.

Until I caught her copying my classwork.

We would both get in trouble if the teacher found out on her own, which was why I told her what had happened. It was the right thing to do, and I don't regret it.

But our teacher contacted Libby's parents. She was banned from tryouts for our school's play, and she was sent to detention for two recesses.

She's been cruel to me ever since.

We're surging down I-5 with our car windows cracked, wind pummeling through the open spaces. Freeway bridges curve in toward the city's heart, the dense, gleaming skyscrapers. The Space Needle looks like a flying saucer with ivory legs rooted in the ground. Seaplanes circle and dive, skimming across Lake Union's blue surface.

Adam has a portable video game console in his lap, his small fingers clicking the buttons impossibly fast. Amelia's mom mutters something profane about drivers not using their turn signals.

"I hate this city," Libby says. "Seattle is so annoying. I can't wait until I graduate from high school and I can move literally anywhere else in the world."

"I kind of like it," Amelia says. "But I can also see why you hate it."

"It's the worst. I want to go someplace that's sunny year-round."

"At least your house is nice!" Amelia looks at me. "You would love Libby's house. She lives on that hill by Golden Gardens. She has the *best* view."

Libby shifts her attention to me. "Do you actually like Golden Gardens?" She scrunches her nose. "Because ew. It gets *so* crowded and gross, especially during the summer."

I stare at her, unsure of what to say.

Amelia clears her throat. Her thin blonde eyebrows are drawn together. She looks annoyed with me. Which is fine, because I'm even more annoyed with her.

Libby asks her, "Does she ever talk?"

Amelia says, "Sometimes."

And now we're exiting the freeway. The shift in direction forces Libby to lean into me; a frustrated

Adam slams his console against his lap. Amelia turns around, her slim ponytail whipping.

The air smells of car exhaust and sun-warmed garbage. It's unpleasant, but I'm grateful for the lack of urine. The last time I came downtown, I could smell pee everywhere.

We're crossing a crowded intersection. The red hand is flashing, urging us to stop, but we keep moving. An elderly, dark-skinned man is playing the saxophone on the street corner. A cardboard sign is propped up by his feet, with the words "Anything helps, God bless" penned in blue ink. Libby and Amelia are in the lead, followed by Amelia's mom and Adam, followed by me. They all zip past the saxophonist without a glance or a coin to spare, so I do, too, even though I don't feel very good about it.

Amelia's mom passes around sticks of chewing gum. She extends one to me, shoving it into my hand before I can decline her offer. I sweep my thumb across the silver wrapper. The gum bends, wilting from the heat of my palm.

We turn down an alley, just below the main entrance to Pike Place Market. The brick walls are covered in posters and stickers, all bright and colorful, abstract and strange. I slow down to stare at the collage. There are grinning skulls; a ghoulish, blue-skinned woman with glowing yellow eyes; a caricature of a great, horned animal; illegible graffiti signatures; advertisements for local bands and theater productions.

And gum.

As we continue down the alley, flecks of gum appear on both sides.

"This is so *cool*," Adam crows as he dashes forward to get a better view.

Amelia shrieks, "*Ewww*." She clasps her hands over her cheeks. "Why do people do this?"

"This is sick," Libby says.

They're all still way ahead of me, so I'm going to assume no one cares to hear my opinion. Since we left the car, Amelia hasn't stood beside me once. She's barely even looked at me. I slow down even more, allowing the gap between us to widen. Just to see if she'll notice.

She doesn't. The Gum Wall has captured her full attention.

An entire stretch of the alleyway is coated in chewed pieces of gum, a sticky, pointillist rainbow across the bricks. A window ledge is covered in stretched, dangling strips that look like melted wax. Someone arranged blue bits into squiggly initials: *JC + CC.*

Adam is the first to pull his gum out of his mouth and stick it to the wall. Libby and Amelia follow, squealing and pushing each other. Except while Amelia pushes playfully, Libby gives her an actual *shove*. Almost like she *wanted* her to fall back against the Gum Wall.

And Amelia seriously wants to be friends with her? I don't understand. Not at all.

"Enough roughhousing," Amelia's mom says. "Let's all pose for a picture now." As an afterthought, she glances at me. "Aren't you going to add to the Gum Wall, Edie?"

I open my mouth to respond, but Amelia's mom cuts me off, eyes bulging.

"Oh!" she cries. "Your braces. I'm so sorry, sweetie, I forgot."

I feel small as I shrug. "It's okay."

Amelia glances at me, but she doesn't apologize for starting our day with an activity I can't participate in. She doesn't apologize for inviting someone else along—a girl who hates me.

When we squeeze together for a picture, Amelia throws one arm around my shoulders and the other around Libby's. As her mom takes the photograph, it might look like she's standing perfectly in the middle. But the truth is, I can feel my best friend pulling away.

19.

THE BUTT OF A BAD JOKE

July 10

Pike Place Market is wild. There are glowing neon signs, fresh-cut wildflowers, fruits and vegetables stacked in bright, shiny rows. Dried chili peppers hang along the eaves, lavender sachets are laced with ribbons, jars filled with homemade jams line the shelves. Various forms of seafood are packed into ice: mussels, their shells as smooth and dark as river rocks; whole crabs, their pincers lifted to the sky; silver salmon, their brilliant scales gleaming under the lights.

One of the seafood workers—a huge man,

dressed in an orange apron—throws an entire salmon across the counter, where it lands in another man's arms with a wet *smack*. Onlookers clap and cheer. But the whole scene reminds me of my conversation with Uncle Phil, about the salmon that didn't return, the empty nets that last year he worked as a fisherman.

Libby and Amelia walk close, their heads bent together so they can hear each other speak through the noise, the chaos. Amelia's mom walks with her cell phone held out, determined to document everything in pictures. Adam darts around, eager for closer looks at everything he can touch.

Bars of soap are brightly fragranced, and colored in soft pastels. Vials are filled with ash from the Mount St. Helen's eruption, and they look like granulated potions, dark glittering magic. Prints of watercolor tulip fields are sheathed in plastic. Glass bear-shaped jars are filled with thick, gold honey.

It's lunchtime, so Amelia's mom guides us toward the row of restaurants and food counters along the opposite side of the street. Adam gets a hot dog, Libby gets a panini from a French bakery, and Amelia insists on going to the cheese place.

The line is long, and the air is humid. Huge windows line one wall, revealing the cheesemaking process, massive machines stirring and churning the creamy cheddar. Amelia and I get the macaroni and cheese. Despite how soft and delicious it is, my teeth still hurt as I eat.

We're gathered around an outdoor picnic table. The wood is covered in bird poop and graffiti scribbles. We hold our food in our laps, not willing to trust the cleanliness of the table. I slurp some macaroni off my spoon and move it gently around inside my mouth. Libby whispers something in Amelia's ear, and Amelia bursts out with this fake laugh.

I tell myself they aren't laughing at me. But I don't fully believe it.

I remember this one day, when I was really little and getting frustrated with Uncle Phil's "I've got your nose!" trick. He sat there laughing, slapping his knee as he cracked himself up.

"Come on, kiddo. You know it's a good joke."

I stood my ground. Shook my head. "I don't like it when you laugh at me."

He immediately sobered. I have no clue how old I was, but I think it was the first time I ever spoke back to Uncle Phil. The first time he realized he was bothering me, when he thought he was just being funny.

"Edie, I'm not laughing *at* you. I would never do that."

"You do it every time I come over."

"I'm trying to make you laugh *with* me. There's a huge difference."

I'd never thought of it like that before. But I still wasn't convinced.

"I make a lot of jokes, but you are never the butt of any of them. I wouldn't make you the butt of a bad joke."

A small snort escaped me. I erupted in giggles.

"What?" he asked. "What's funny now?"

"You said the B-word."

His eyes bulged. "What? Butt?"

"Uncle Phil! You said it again." I laughed so hard, it felt like my sides were splitting.

Uncle Phil chuckled, too. "Oh, is that so? You think the B-word is pretty funny, huh? How about the F-word?"

I gasped, wide-eyed.

He pressed the heels of his hands against his mouth and made the loudest farting noise I'd ever heard.

That day, we both laughed together so hard, we cried.

"*Edie.* Hello? Earth to Edie."

I flinch at the sound of Amelia's voice and realize I've been zoning out. Everyone else is finished with their lunch, and they're waiting on me. Meanwhile, my cup of macaroni and cheese is still nearly full.

I gulp. "Sorry. It's hard for me to eat with my braces."

"Seriously?" Amelia snaps. "It's mac and cheese, Edie. It's like the softest food you can get."

"It's not my fault."

Amelia's mom says, "Take your time, Edie. We're not in any hurry. And, Amelia, you better quit that tone and apologize, young lady. Have some empathy for your friend."

Amelia's face turns a bright, angry red from her mother's scolding. She narrows her eyes at me.

"I don't *hear* an apology. You've already lost five minutes from your screen time today. The longer it takes, the more you'll lose."

Adam cackles at his sister. Libby looks at me and smirks.

Amelia grinds the words out painfully, like

they're scratching the inside of her throat. "I'm sorry for being mean to you, Edie. I'm sure you must be hurting. Take as long as you want."

I finally understand what Uncle Phil meant. He never made me the butt of a bad joke. This is what that feels like.

20.

SAY A PRAYER FOR THEM

July 10

That was the worst trip downtown in history. I
don't think anyone has ever been so miserable at
Pike Place Market.

"Thanks so much for joining us, Edie," Amelia's
mom says as we arrive at my house. "Hope to see
you again soon."

"Thanks."

Amelia and I don't have anything to say to each
other. I unbuckle my seat belt, Libby climbs out of
the car, and I squeeze past her through the open
door.

Libby smirks at me. "See you around."

I don't have anything to say to her, either. I just shove my hands into my pockets and cross my front yard with dread pooling in my stomach.

Mom opens the front door for me and waves goodbye as their car pulls away from the curb.

"Hey," she says. Her voice is bright and cheerful. "Did you girls have fun?"

I head straight for the kitchen, avoiding eye contact and her arms, which are opening for a hug.

Mom flinches, surprised. "Edie?"

I shrug and head straight for the kitchen. She follows me, a little cautiously.

"Is everything okay?"

"Everything is fine." I open the fridge and am met with a rush of cool air against my skin. There are packages of grapes and tomatoes, blocks of cheese, cartons of milk and juice.

"Are you hungry, sweetheart? Should I make you a sandwich?"

I sigh and close the fridge door. "I can't eat stuff like that right now, Mom. I had a hard enough time eating mac and cheese." My voice breaks awkwardly on the word *cheese*, and I duck my head, shielding my face behind a curtain of hair.

"Really?" Mom asks, sudden and concerned. "That painful?"

"What do you think?" I mutter. "I hate having braces."

She steps aside for me as I leave the kitchen and start typing a message to Serenity.

Serenity? Hello? Do you have service yet?

I hit send and immediately write another.

I really need to talk to you. Are you friends with Libby now, too? Did you know she and Amelia have been hanging out? You can tell me.

I push through my bedroom door and flop down on the bed. My back is to her, but I can sense my mother standing in the doorway, watching me.

"I'm sorry they're bothering you, sweetie." She pauses. Waits. "Is there anything I can do to help you? Anything else you want to tell me?"

I press my face against the pillow. Shake my head.

"Okay," she murmurs. "Let me know if you change your mind."

She waits for a moment. Then her footsteps retreat down the hall.

Serenity still hasn't responded to my texts. But Amelia sent a few of her own.

Amelia: You didn't have to be so rude to her, you know. She's actually really nice.

Amelia: And she wants to help us with the film! She can draw the people, while you draw the background stuff.

Amelia: It would be cool if you texted me back.

Amelia: Are you giving me the silent treatment?

I plug the phone into my charger and walk over to the closet. Remove the art chest. Pull the folded letter free from my pocket. Tuck it back inside the box.

Her smiling face peeks at me. There are so many copies of her head shots. I wonder how many she had, how many she gave away. I start to pick through her letters again, looking for the next one she wrote. It takes me a little while, but I find it:

March 16, 1974

Dear Theo,

Hello! I hope you are well. How's work? How's Mom? Please give her the biggest hug from me.

You will not believe what has recently happened. I've landed two more roles, both in upcoming films with Paramount Pictures. They're minor, uncredited parts, which felt like a setback after having spoken lines in my first film. But my agent keeps insisting that many actors go through moments like these before they land supporting and lead roles. The important thing is to be around, to let people see your face in multiple settings. To let them recognize you and wonder, "Gosh, where have I seen her before?"

Ultimately, I feel okay with being in the background for now. After all, I'm still so new here. I'm working hard in my acting classes, and I also spend a lot of time reading scripts and monologues alone in my apartment. I think I might buy myself a video recorder, so I can watch footage of myself as I practice. I'd also like to spend more time in front of a camera, so that I get used to the sensation of being taped. In the first film, I found it quite difficult to ignore the camera as it was pointed at me. I need to reach a point where being recorded feels like nothing.

Anyways, that's enough about the acting thing. I must admit, I'm homesick. It's lonely being the only Indian woman around. Every single day, someone walks up to me in the restaurant, or they stop me on the street and ask, "Where are you from?" At least, those are the polite ones. Just the other day, someone threw a bag of trash at me from their car, and drove off laughing.

I'm sorry if these anecdotes make you angry. I promise, I really am okay. I just wanted to get that stuff off my chest, because it's starting to grate on me. It's a difficult life, trying to live on your own, away from your family and community, in a city known for being cutthroat.

Please don't worry, big brother. Some people might refuse to show me kindness now, but I will find a way into their hearts. And if their hearts still won't open in the future, I won't be discouraged. I won't let them keep me down.

I will simply say a prayer for them, and move on.

Love,
Edith

I release a hard, shuddering breath.

The lawn mower starts up somewhere outside, but it sounds distant, faraway. Like I'm hearing it through the opposite end of a long, dark tunnel.

21.

AND MOVE ON

July 11

Amelia was my first best friend. We met during recess in kindergarten. She was perched on top of the monkey bars, and I was walking along the woodchips.

"Hey!" Amelia called out. "You! Do you know how to get up here?"

I stopped and shrugged. Which was my own shy version of saying, *No*.

"It's super easy. Come here, I'll show you."

She jumped down, her skirt ballooning as she soared through the air. She was wearing a red-and-white-checked dress, with frilly white socks and black ballet flats. Her hair was pulled back in a messy ponytail, blonde strands springing free in every direction.

When she hit the ground, she ran toward me with a goofy grin. She grabbed my hand and led me to the ladder. She went first, demonstrating how to swing out to the middle, before she brought her knees to her chest, hooked her legs over the bar's edge, and pulled herself up to a seated position.

"See? Piece of cake."

I followed her, since she made it look so easy. I had a hard time pulling myself up, so she reached down to help me. Her palm was warm and clammy, but I didn't mind at all. Especially once I was up there beside her.

"Best view of the playground," Amelia said coolly. She threw her arm around my shoulders, cementing our friendship. "And now we can hang out whenever and wherever we want to."

I'm walking to Amelia's house. I left my bike there yesterday, in her front yard. I come around the corner and there it is, sprawled in the short grass.

She must sense my approach, because the front door opens right away. She peeks at me through the gap. Her brows are pulled together.

"Well," she says. "Did you see what I said about having Libby in the film with us? I think she'd be great."

I had an entire speech planned out in my head. But suddenly, I can't remember how to start it. The words I chose.

Amelia steps forward, into the middle of the doorway. Her pupils narrow into slits. "Are you going to talk to me today? Or were you planning on just grabbing your bike and leaving without a word?"

Heat floods through my veins. "How long have you been friends with her?" My voice cracks as I speak. "Why didn't you tell me?"

"So, we've known her forever, and I thought it would be cool to hang out with her. She used to hang out with us, a long time ago."

My hands wobble into fists at my sides. I feel my chin tremble. "She's not a good person, Amelia. Remember when she cheated off of my work? When she became friends with Madison, and they followed me around at recess, making all kinds of mean jokes?" Even as I say these words, I know it's pointless. Because I've told her about Libby. She *knows* what she's like.

And she wants to be friends with her anyways.

"You didn't even talk to her yesterday," Amelia says. "People grow up. They change."

"Libby is a bully," I whisper. "She always has been."

"Not to me. She seems so nice. I can't imagine her being mean to anyone for no reason."

For no reason. What's that supposed to mean?

I scuff my shoe against the grass. "I don't want her involved in the film," I admit quietly. "I'm not comfortable with that. And I also don't think we should draw inspiration from the other Edith. It doesn't seem right."

Amelia looks shocked. She crosses her arms over her chest. "Excuse me?" she says. "What do you mean it 'doesn't seem right'?"

"We don't know her full story. Not really. And even if we did, all that stuff was her real life. We can't just create a film based on her life, without her permission. That would be wrong."

I lift my chin. This was the main part of the speech I'd planned. I've been wanting to tell Amelia how I feel about this. I'm glad it's finally off my chest.

"It won't be the exact same," Amelia argues. "We're not going to *plagiarize* her. Filmmakers create stories based on true events all the time. It's a common thing."

"Just because other people do it, that doesn't mean we should."

Amelia throws her hands up. "You're making this a much bigger deal than it should be," she says. "But whatever. I'm the director, but I guess I don't get to have an opinion. What should our story be about, then?"

Her anger makes me flinch. Still, I steel myself and tell her, "The dog."

"The dog. Seriously?"

"Yes. It's what Serenity and I have wanted from the beginning."

"Even though it would be boring? And predictable?"

"It wouldn't be either of those things."

She rolls her eyes. "Sure."

I'm trying to stay calm, but it's hard. "What has gotten into you?" I ask. "Why are you being like this?"

"I don't know, Edie. I'm just sick of this."

"Of what?"

"Literally everything. I really don't like the dog idea. I don't think it's very creative, and I don't think it will be good enough to win any prizes."

"So that's what you care about? The grand prize at the festival?"

"It's what we should *all* be thinking about! What's the point of entering, if we don't want to win?"

There's a huge lump lodged in my throat. This isn't going to work. I can't make her choose the dog. I can't make her choose me.

A part of me wishes Libby was here. I would have no problem telling her to get lost.

But it's just the two of us—Amelia and me. Former best friends, who now seem to be going down different paths.

"If that's how you feel—" I pause. Swallow. "Y-you can leave our group. You and Libby can work on something else."

There's a brief, stunned silence. Then her voice is cold as ice as she says, "Well. That sounds perfectly fine by me."

And that's all I can stand to hear.

I lift and mount my bike.

As I push the pedals and the chain whirs back to life, she shouts: "It's better this way! Now we won't be limited to animation. We can film ourselves and act it out, the way *I've* wanted to from the beginning."

Her words spear through me. They cut me down.

I surge through the streets to my house, racing the tears before they have a chance to fall.

22.

THE MOST SHOCKING THING OF ALL

July 11

My eyes are red and puffy. I can taste salt on my lips, and wisps of hair are sticking to my sweaty forehead.

I think I'm out of tears by now.

I'd like to believe I made the right choice. But I'm not sure if that's true. At least, not yet.

Amelia chose Libby. She is no longer the friend I thought she was. I see that now. I can see it in the time stamps from our text messages. I can hear it in our different opinions about the film festival. Yesterday, I felt it during our time together at Pike

Place Market. And if I'm being really honest, I think I felt it several times before then.

Even so, she has always been one of my favorite people. And if our friendship is over, it will be hard to move forward. It will be hard to let her go.

I wipe the back of my hand across my warm, wet eyelids.

Check my phone for notifications.

Still nothing from Serenity. I wonder why that is. A knock sounds at my door. Mom opens it, sticks her head in.

"Hey," she says. I'm not sure if she knows I've been crying. If she does, she pretends not to. "What are you up to?"

I tell her, "Nothing."

"No plans with your friends tonight?"

I shake my head.

"Hmm. Okay. Maybe we should have our own girls' night. Just the two of us. How does that sound?"

I mumble, "Sure."

"We could go to Golden Gardens," she says. "Catch the sunset, get some ice cream."

My heart aches at the thought of drawing. Of working on my favorite landscape, or my sweet little dog. Under normal circumstances, nothing would make me happier. But right now, my heart just wouldn't be in it.

"Don't feel like it."

"No?" She sounds surprised, but quickly skips ahead to her next suggestion. "Why don't we go see a movie, then? Would that be fun?"

"Sure."

"Wonderful!" Mom says. "I'll look up movie times and we'll go."

She leaves my bedroom door open, and I check my phone for notifications again, even though it's been less than a minute.

Goose bumps prickle along my arms as we enter the cinema. The air inside the building is cool; the lobby is empty and dim. The black carpet is patterned with colorful geometric shapes. Small light bulbs are tucked between the ceiling tiles. One wall is lined with movie posters and cardboard character cutouts. The other end of the room boasts the concessions: glass-paneled and red-topped popcorn machines, shelves stacked with boxes of candy, empty plastic cups piled between the cash registers and soda fountains.

In the far corner of the lobby, a glass door leads to a private room. That was where we celebrated Amelia's sixth birthday. We all dressed up in costumes, as characters in the movie we watched together. And we ate lots of yellow cake and buttered popcorn. Amelia always had the best birthday parties: movies, bowling, ice-skating. Her birthday is in November—the gloomiest month of the year—but that never stopped her from planning something fun.

But as of today, I might never celebrate a birthday with her again.

"This movie is going to be so cute!" Mom says gleefully as we stride past a cutout display of animated characters. They're depicted in bright colors and bold, sweeping lines. I can't help but admire the attention to detail, the expressiveness in their eyes.

"Do you want anything to drink? We could also check to see if they have any snacks you could eat."

"Um, I'm not really—"

I pause mid-sentence, mid-step.

"Edie? What are you—?" She sees what I see and comes to an abrupt stop. "Oh."

A movie poster has captured my attention.

I'm not sure what this film is about. I've never heard of it before. It might be an action-adventure film. Or a Western. Or something else entirely.

But one of the characters is a Native American woman.

"Wow," I say. "This looks awesome."

Mom shifts on her feet. She looks around, apparently uncomfortable.

But the woman on the poster—she looks so proud, so regal. She has red face paint smeared over her eyes. She's wearing an orange headband with a single feather attached to it, and her deer-skin clothing is fringed with beaded tassels.

And her eyes are blue. That's the most shocking thing of all.

"I didn't know Native Americans could have blue eyes."

Mom's gaze snaps back to me; she looks startled.

"Did you know that was possible?" I ask.

"Yes. Some do," she says. "But—" She looks at the poster. Shakes her head a little, then looks away. "Come on, Edie. We don't want to be late for the movie."

I can't keep my eyes off the poster. All I can think about is Edith Graham, leaving her home and her family to pursue a career in acting. I think about her courage, her kindness, her determination. I think how homesick she was, how much she sacrificed just to get small roles.

I wonder if this woman has a similar story. I wonder where she's from.

"Could we actually watch this, instead?"

"Erm, no, sweetheart. I don't think so."

"How come?"

She's so uncomfortable. I can feel it. And I know there must be a reason for it, a full explanation.

But she decides to hide it.

"We already have tickets for *Hannah and Blue*," she says. "I thought we were both excited to see it. Let's just stick to the original plan, okay?"

She starts to walk away, but I stand my ground and ask, "What if I changed my mind? What if I really want to see this now?"

Her purse slides off her shoulder, and she hikes it back up. She keeps her body angled away from the poster. Like she can't bear to look at it. "Edie," she says softly. "I think I know why you want to see this other movie. And I know you're upset. But please, trust my judgment."

"I'm not *upset*. I just want to see this movie."

She sighs as she turns to face me. "I know what you're thinking," she says. "That this film might be able to show you something. That you might learn something from it about your heritage." She looks sad as she says this. Distraught, even. "But you need to listen to me: a film like that won't give you what you're looking for."

"You don't know that," I huff. "You haven't even seen it."

"Indeed. Looking at the poster is more than enough for me. What you need to und—"

"The poster? What's wrong with the poster?"

"Calm down, Edie. Please, just let me—"

"Don't tell me to calm down! At least this movie would show me *something*." My arms are crossed over my chest, and my voice is filled with venom, and I know I'm being mean and unfair, but the words still come out: "That's a lot more than I could say about *you*."

Mom reels back, as if my words have landed with the force of an actual, physical blow.

I release a hard, sharp breath. My throat feels scraped and raw.

I've hurt her. I know that. I know I've made a huge mistake, that I shouldn't have raised my voice, but I'm her daughter. I deserve to know as much as she knows.

I deserve to know the meaning of my own name.

Mom's face contorts with pain. She cups one hand over her mouth. Drags it down to the edge of her chin. Her knuckles turn white with strain. "Okay," she murmurs. She sucks in a deep breath and lets it out. "Okay," she says again. "Maybe we shouldn't do this today. I'll return the tickets. And we'll go home." She licks her lips. Nods. "I'll take you home."

This might be the worst day of my life.

Everything is ruined with Amelia. Everything is ruined with my mom.

And I'm pretty sure it's all my fault.

Dad's car is parked in the driveway at home. When we walk through the front door, he's there, sitting with his elbows on his knees on the living room couch. He has potato chips and sour-cream-and-onion dip on the coffee table. A baseball game is playing on the TV.

"My girls!" Dad throws his arms open. "Where have you been? Want some chips and dip? It's a great game tonight; we're ahead two to nothin'."

I give him a weak smile and ignore the invitation for a hug. At least someone I love is having a good day. I wouldn't want to ruin his mood, too.

Which is why I say nothing, and head straight to my room.

23.

LITTLE BUN

July 11

When I try calling Serenity, it immediately goes to voicemail. Either her phone is off, or she has no service. Not that this makes me feel any better. Nothing feels good right now.

Except maybe this.

I kneel before the box. Open its flaps. Reach inside.

I pluck several postcards out. I haven't really looked at these yet, only the notes she wrote to Theo. The first one says *Greetings from California* in big, bold letters. Each letter outlines an image:

an orange grove, a turquoise stretch of beach, a curved road. Another appears to be from Los Angeles, with silhouetted illustrations of a movie camera, and the Hollywood Hills.

I flip them over and skim the short messages:

October 16, 1973

Dear Mom and Theo,

    I've arrived! Southern California is warm and grand and beautiful. I wish you could see these beaches with me. I know you'd love this coast as much as I do.

    Hugs,

    Edith

November 21, 1975

Dear Mom and Theo,

    I hope you enjoy this gorgeous postcard. I'm using it as bait for you both to come down and visit me! (It's a difficult situation, I know. But a girl can dream.)

    With love,

    Edith

These sweet messages make me smile.

I set the first two aside and dig through the box to find her other postcards.

As I sift through this stuff, a realization hits: I no longer have to keep the box a secret from my parents. It was Amelia's idea to hide the discovery from them, and now that we're no longer friends, I can ask Mom and Dad about it. I can bring it up whenever I want.

If I want.

I'm not even sure.

Everything is changing so fast, and after our fight at the movie theater, I don't know how Mom would react if she found out the box is here, in my room. That I've been keeping it in my art chest, reading these letters by myself in the dark.

Will Mom be mad? Will she be upset? Is it even possible for her to tell me the truth now?

Uncle Phil said that she and Dad were going to tell me about Edith Graham. He knew who she was, and he seemed confident that I only needed to be "old enough." Whatever that's supposed to mean.

I gather the postcards in a little pile and tap the edges against the floor, lining them up.

Almost all of them have pictures of Los Angeles.

Palm trees and sorbet-flavored sunsets. Spotlights and skyscrapers.

But then, randomly, I find one from San Francisco. It shows the Golden Gate Bridge, stretched over the bright blue water.

Curious, I flip this one over.

February 13, 1977

Dear Mom and Theo,

> *Brief stop in SF. The bus for Seattle leaves tomorrow afternoon. Little Bun and I are on our way home!*
>
> *All my love,*
> *Edith*

My grip tightens reflexively. I accidentally bend the card, forming a crease down the middle as I read and reread these three sentences. I keep getting caught up by the same phrase.

Little Bun and I.
Little Bun and I.
Little Bun and I.

Who is she talking about? Why is she leaving Hollywood? What *happened*?

Frantic, I start yanking her letters out of the box, checking the dates, scanning each page for potential hints. Over the past few days, her handwriting has become familiar, easier to read. But regardless, some of these collapsed loops and hasty scribbles are impossible to make out.

In a message from October 1976, I think she tells Theo: *I feel so foolish. I never should have come here.* But the rest of that paragraph is illegible.

Did she have regrets? What was going on in her career?

In another one from March 1975, she says: *They edited most of my lines out of the final cut. Now I only say two words in the film, and the entire story is so different. It's no longer the positive, sensitive picture I signed up for. They decided to change it, because they think a "more classic" Western will sell better at the box office. I wish I'd never agreed to any of this. They've broken all their promises.*

And in December 1975: *It's easy to be discouraged. I've always considered myself to be an optimistic person. But some days, I can't make myself be happy and keep working hard, for a dream that might never materialize. Some days, it's hard to remember why I'm doing any of it.*

No, I want to say. I want to reach for the girl behind these letters and give her a hug. I want to tell her not to give up on her dreams.

She sounds so lost, all of a sudden. She sounds alone and afraid.

I hope it doesn't stay that way.

And then:

January 1, 1977

Dear Family,

I'm coming home.

I've purchased my bus tickets and arranged travel plans for mid–February. I do not plan on returning to California. Although I ultimately don't regret these past few years, I've come to the realization that this is not the place for me. I belong in Suquamish, with all of you. I belong in my homelands, with my loved ones.

Now that I've gotten a taste of the world beyond our little corner of the Puget Sound, I can safely say that venturing out on your own is overrated. It's fine to try and change the world. To define yourself as an activist, an artist, an individual. But solo adventures can only last for so long. The journey is always better together. And I've missed you all so much.

As you might have guessed, however, my

homesickness isn't my only motivation here. It's also true that I've given up on trying to act, and on the relationships I've built here. This includes my job, my acting classes, the unions I've joined, etc. It also includes a man, whom I've never told you about. And whom I still feel reluctant to tell you about, although it is impossible to deny his existence now.

Because I'm pregnant with his child.

Yes, you read that correctly. I'm expecting a baby. The father will not be in the picture when I come home, and I think it will be best this way. But here we are. Our family is growing a little bigger this year.

I already know that becoming a mother will be the greatest joy of my life. From the moment I found out, I realized this is what I'm meant to be. The leading role I'm meant to have.

The tears are coming hard and fast, so I'll wrap this letter up for now. Just please know that I have no regrets about any of this. I'm so excited to meet my baby. I can't wait to see the baby's face, to kiss their cheeks, to tickle their tiny toes.

Now that I've landed this role, I'm amazed I ever wanted anything else.

Love,
Edith

24.

PICKLE JUICE

July 12

I barely slept at all last night.

Mom places an orange bowl on the table before me. The bowl is filled with a purple liquid, thick and textured and rich, riddled with tiny bits of seeds. Banana slices are balanced on its surface, arranged in the shape of a smiley face. Coconut shavings are sprinkled above the top two slices, in wide crescents that look like eyebrows.

"Thanks."

"You're welcome." She glances at me. She looks worried and tense, and I know she's thinking about last night. About our fight at the movie theater. "How are your teeth feeling this morning?"

I press a fingertip against my swollen lips. "Better."

"Think you can get around some buttered toast?"

"I can try."

She sets a small turquoise plate beside the bowl. Two slices of sourdough toast. Slightly browned and buttered, just how I like them.

"If your teeth are still too sore, let me know. But it's been a few days. Dr. Ashworth seemed to think you'd be more adjusted by now." Mom sits across from me. Her brows are knitted together with concern. "I'm starting to worry."

I pick up a slice of toast and bite the crusted corner. Overall, my teeth really are better. I can smile and brush my teeth without any real consequences. But I still experience shooting pains whenever I chew.

"It's okay," I say. I set the bread aside and grab my spoon.

Mom watches me as I eat. Dad strides in, takes his seat at the table. He's dressed for work in a crisp shirt and tie, a fancy watch flashing at his wrist. He and Mom are both eating smoothie bowls for breakfast, too. In solidarity, I guess. For several minutes, no one says anything. The only sounds in here are the slow, repetitive clanks of our spoons.

Then Dad pipes up with "Have we ever told you about your mother's weird pregnancy cravings?"

I gulp. Shake my head.

"Two words: pickle juice."

Mom smirks. "That was random, Donnie."

"I'm just saying. It was a total thing. I was at the grocery store almost every day, getting fresh dill pickles for you."

"But Mom doesn't even like pickles."

Dad slaps the tabletop. "Yes! That's *exactly* my point—"

"I don't *dislike* them. It's just—I don't know. They're not as satisfying, now that I'm no longer craving them."

The conversation fizzles out awkwardly. I chase a banana slice around inside my bowl. Mom and Dad are nearly finished with theirs.

And the words fly out of me: "I know where my name came from."

Everything stops. Their spoons go still. Their eyes fix on me.

It's like I temporarily lost control of my own mouth. But now that the confession is out there, I might as well keep going.

So I look at Mom and say, "Your biological mother's name was Edith Graham. She was from here, but she wanted to become an actress. She left for Hollywood in 1973, and she came back to Seattle when she was pregnant with you. You were born on August 28, 1977."

Mom holds my gaze. She blinks a few times, her eyelids fluttering.

"She had an older brother named Theo. She had a gap between her two front teeth. She was inspired by someone named Sacheen. She took acting lessons, and she worked hard, even though she never got any good parts. But none of it mattered when she realized she was going to be a mother. From then on, all she wanted was you."

My voice wavers and cracks. I think of Amelia, who didn't want me to do this. I think of Serenity and Uncle Phil, who thought I should have done it from the beginning.

"What happened to her? Why were you adopted?"

I stop. I wait to see who was right. I wait to see what my parents will do now.

Dad speaks first: "You found the box." He chuckles. Looks down at his hands. "I don't know why we even bother hiding things from you. We could never keep birthday or Christmas gifts a secret. You always found what you were getting." He checks his watch. Glances at Mom. "I have an appointment with a client this morning. But I can take the rest of the day off, if you're ready to tell Edie everything. We can take her there," he says, "like we always wanted to."

My breath catches. I look at her, silently pleading.

And she says, "Okay."

Triumph blazes through me. I feel tears well in my eyes, but they aren't like happy tears, or even sad tears. I think these might be tears of relief.

Dad says, "Great. I'll be back as soon as I can."

Before he leaves, he walks behind my chair, wraps his arms around me, and presses a kiss to the top of my head. "My sweet girl," he says. "You're my entire world. You know that, right?"

I nod. "I know, Dad."

"Good." He kisses my head again, then grabs his sport coat and goes to work.

Mom is quiet as she rinses the bowls and places

them in the dishwasher. She also washes the blender she used, scrubbing and wiping it down until the plastic is clear and shiny. When she sets it on the drying rack beside the sink, she says, "I had a feeling. Ever since I found you girls in the attic, I knew there was . . . *something.*"

I swallow. "Are you mad?"

"No, sweetie. I would never be mad at you for being curious. I'd never be mad at you for wanting to know where your name came from, where *we* came from. I just—I wish I would've had a little more control, in this situation. I wish I could have shown you those letters and photographs myself."

So Uncle Phil was right. She really was planning on showing me the box someday.

"I'm sorry, Mom."

"Please don't apologize. There's nothing to be sorry for."

"For last night," I tell her sheepishly. "I'm sorry I said those things at the theater. I didn't mean any of it."

She smiles. Takes a step toward me. "That reminds me," she says. "I need you to understand why I didn't want to see that movie. I . . . sort of choked up when you asked about it. And I wish I would have done better. I wish would've composed myself, and explained it to you right away, instead of avoiding the discussion."

Parents can be weird. Serenity's words ring in my head. *They make mistakes. But they're not try-ing to hurt you, Edie.*

"It's okay," I say softly. "I'm not mad."

"I'm glad to hear it. Do you remember the actress on the poster?"

I nod.

"She wasn't a real Native. That actress's name is Léa Lejeune. She's originally from Belgium. In that movie, she's supposed to be an 'Indian prin-cess,' so she dyed her hair black and wore that awful costume."

"Oh."

"Yes. Movies like that show Native people as something exotic and mythical, but there is no truth to them. That was not a real Native woman. Her outfit had no cultural significance. Everything about it was fake and Hollywoodized, for the sake of making a profit."

"In that case, I guess I'm glad we didn't see it."

"Me too."

Mom looks out the window. It's open a few

inches, just enough to let a breeze in. The white cotton curtains swell and sway, the folds rippling slightly.

"Mom?"

"Hmm?"

"Where are we going, after Dad comes home from his appointment?"

She breathes in deep. Turns to face me. "Indianola," she says. "We're taking you to Indianola. And along the way, we'll explain everything about that box. There will be no more secrets. No more surprises."

25.

AN OTHER IN YOUR OWN FAMILY

July 12

I sit in the lawn chair in our backyard while Mom pulls her garden gloves on. My drawing pad is open in my lap, and my pencil is idling in my hand, the eraser tap-tap-tapping against the corner of the page.

"Do we have to wait until Dad comes home?" I ask.

Mom chuckles. "To go to Indianola?"

"To talk about Edith Graham."

Her shoulders stiffen. She keeps her face turned slightly away from me. Then she seems to suck in a breath and release it slowly.

"Your father should be a part of that conversation. But if you want, I can tell you a little more about me. And my childhood. And the reasons why I felt compelled to find her."

"That sounds good." I flip my sketchbook shut and lean forward, placing my elbows on my knees. "You never tell me stories from when you were growing up."

She laughs again, in earnest this time. She flexes her fingers and kneels before her garden bed. "That's because I never wanted you to feel sorry for me."

I'm not sure what to say to that. She yanks a weed and continues to speak.

"I was put up for adoption the day I was born. If you look at my original birth certificate, you'll find that I didn't even have a name when I first came into the world. Eventually, in the orphanage, they named me Lisa. Your grandparents found me at six months old, and that was when I legally became Lisa Miller.

"I still wish you could have met your grandma and grandpa Miller. They loved telling the story of that day they found me. Grandma Miller swore she knew I was the one for her right away. She said that I smiled at her, toothless and jolly. And when she took me in her arms, she wouldn't let them take me back. She held on, and she never let go.

"Phil didn't like me too much, at first." She giggles, remembering. "He was used to being an only child, and he was a bit of a brat back then. As I'm sure you can imagine."

"He's definitely still a brat."

"True. Anyways, when I was very young, he teased me all the time. I convinced myself that he hated me, like many of the kids in our neighborhood." She pauses. Licks her lips. "I was the only Native American person around, you see. I always knew I was Native, though my parents didn't know which tribe I came from, or who my biological family was. They knew I was born in Seattle, but that was the extent of their information."

"Do you know which tribe you're from now?"

Her gaze is soft as she turns to me. "Yes. I'm getting there, Edie."

"Oh, okay. Sorry for interrupting."

"It's fine, sweetie. So you see, sometimes people don't know how to act around those they see as different. I remember being bullied all throughout elementary school, especially in middle school. The kids in my grade used to say I needed a bath, because my brown skin looked dirty to them. They spoke to me 'in Indian,' which to them meant wailing and flapping their hands over their mouths. They chased me on their bikes and threw rocks at me.

"All of this—and more—went on for weeks, before Phil found out. He was an eighth grader and I was a fifth grader. I was riding home from school on my bike, trying to avoid the kids who bullied me. While I was coming down the street, a squirrel darted out in front of me, and I swerved so hard to avoid it, I fell off my bike. I skinned my knee and rolled my ankle. The kids were coming fast, cheering and yelling, and I knew I couldn't outrun them. And it was terrifying. I had no idea what they'd do to me.

"But then, quite literally out of nowhere, Phil swooped in on his own bike. He roared and took his stand by my side. He said if anyone wanted to hurt his sister, they'd have to go through him. He used some colorful, inappropriate language, which I will not repeat now. But it worked. He scared the other kids so badly, they all spun around and rode home.

"Once they were gone, Phil helped me to my feet. He knelt down to inspect my knee. He asked me, 'Who were those losers? How long has this been going on?' And when I told him the truth, he could hardly believe it. He asked, 'Why didn't you ever tell me?' And I said, 'I didn't think that you cared.'"

I find my voice and say, "Mom, of course he cared. He's your brother."

She smiles. "I know that now. I wasn't so sure of it then. But I remember that day, because I haven't questioned his love ever since. I was in too much pain to ride my bike, so he helped me walk it back to our house. He disinfected the scrape on my knee and gave me an ice pack for my ankle. From that day on, he always rode his bike alongside me, to and from school. He never let me go alone, and those kids never chased me again."

I can't help but grin. "Yeah," I say. "That sounds like him."

"He has a good heart. He's always been there for me."

She falls silent for a moment. The alder tree in our backyard shimmers with a gust of wind. A hummingbird flits into view with its bejeweled magenta-green chest, its whirring wings.

Finally, she says, "So—in elementary and middle school, I was the only Native person in my neighborhood. But that changed when I got to high school." She yanks another weed free, its thin roots wilting in her grasp. "There was one other Native person. His name was Todd, and he was two grades above me. He was also adopted by white parents, except he knew his Native family. He was placed in foster care when he was five, and he lived in a few different homes before his parents formally took him in, so he always looked and felt like an outsider. I knew exactly what that was like. How it felt to be the only one. How it felt to be an Other in your own family, your own community.

"I tried to be friends with him, but to be honest, our friendship didn't last very long. He was a miserable person to be around. He was sullen and lonely and just generally angry at the world. I felt sorry for him. I knew he was bullied a lot, and I knew his adoptive parents weren't exactly stellar citizens."

"What do you mean?"

"Well. Various reasons. I remember he wanted to grow his hair out, keep it styled in long braids and ponytails. But his parents forced him to keep it buzzed. Stuff like that."

"That's weird. Who cares if a boy wants to have long hair?"

Mom shrugs. "Good question. But they certainly cared. And I remember the explanation he gave me. One day in the lunchroom, he told me, 'They just don't want me to be proud of my heritage. They want me to forget where I came from.'

"That conversation we had really stuck with me. My first reaction was 'Gosh. Why would his own parents not want him to embrace his heritage?' And my second thought was 'Wow. I know absolutely nothing about my cultural background.' I realized I had no idea what it truly meant to be a Native person. I couldn't stop wondering about who my biological parents were, what tribe they were from, or why I was adopted in the first place. Did I end up in that orphanage because something had happened to them? Or did they send me there because I was unwanted? These questions haunted me for years."

Before Mom continues, the sliding glass door opens behind me. Dad pokes his head out. "Hey," he says. "Is everyone having a good day?" He's still in his fancy work clothes, but the tie is loose around his neck. His shirtsleeves are rumpled and rolled up to his elbows.

Mom grins and says, "We are. How are you? How was the meeting?"

"Not too bad. I'm going to go change real quick, before we head out."

"Sounds good, honey."

Dad ducks back inside, and Mom glances at me. She claps her hands, clearing the dirt from them as she stands up. I shift uncomfortably in my chair.

"What happened to Todd?" I ask. "Did his parents get any nicer? Did he grow his hair out as an adult?" I pause. Swallow. "Did he ever reconnect with his family?"

Mom grimaces. "I'm not sure if he ever saw his Native family again. He dropped out of high school, and we lost track of each other for a few years. But while I was still working at the coffeeshop—"

I perk up. "The same place where you met Dad?"

"Yes, the one in the U District. On my way home one night, I crossed paths with Todd at the bus stop. He seemed much happier then. His hair was grown out past his shoulders, and he had a little sparkle in his eye that had never been there before. He gave me a big hug, and he told me everything he'd been up to. He'd earned his GED and he was in school to become an auto mechanic. He was also working as a volunteer, to help immigrants and refugees in the Seattle area, which became his true passion." She smiles at me. "He found his calling. He was really happy."

Todd's happy ending warms me up, from the inside out.

I hope Edith Graham gets one, too.

26.
THE FERRY

July 12

Ten minutes later, the three of us are in Dad's car, driving north on I-5.

Dad has changed into his regular clothes, and he looks much more comfortable. He's in a white button-up and brown khakis, his eyes shielded behind aviator sunglasses. Mom changed her outfit before we left, too. She's wearing a pretty emerald-green sundress.

I scoot forward in my seat and ask, "Where exactly is Indianola?"

"Suquamish territory," Mom answers. "Across

the water from here."

"What's 'Suquamish'?"

"That's who we are," she says. "That's where we're from."

Who we are. Where we're from.

Those two sentences steal my breath.

"But, technically speaking, Suquamish villages were built on both sides of the Sound. So their reservation is across from us, but this whole region counts as our ancestral territory."

"So we're Suquamish. That's what our tribe is called?"

"We're Suquamish *and* Duwamish, actually. Just like Chief Seattle. He signed the Treaty of Point Elliott on behalf of both tribes." Mom catches my gaze in the rearview mirror. "Do you remember studying geography in school?" she asks me. "Do you remember what the European continent looks like?"

I nod.

"Can you imagine how many countries there were?"

I nod again, picturing it in my mind. All those brightly colored patches. Countries of all sizes. Borders drawn in squiggly lines.

"North America is exactly like that. There are countless tribal nations throughout this land. In Washington State alone, there are more than thirty tribes."

"*Really?*"

"Yes. Some are federally recognized—the Suquamish, the Tulalip, the Muckleshoot. Others aren't—the Duwamish, the Chinook, the Snohomish."

"I didn't know Snohomish was a tribe," I say. "I thought that was just the name of the town up north."

"It's a tribe, too," Mom confirms. "They also signed the Treaty of Point Elliott."

"Wow."

I'm straining against my seat belt, waiting to hear more, when my phone buzzes in my pocket. My fingers fumble as I pull it out and unlock the new message.

I gasp at the sight of Serenity's name.

Serenity: hey! sorry service is really spotty and my phone is on the verge of death. your msgs are downloading. i can't read them yet so idk what's up with you, but i hope everything is okay. dad and i are still in the woods, but heading home soon. rly hope this text sends. miss u!

I clutch the phone in both hands. I was so afraid she was ignoring me, but she just couldn't contact me! I'm so relieved, I could cry.

Me: Serenity! Sorry for all the messages. I'm okay, but it's definitely been weird without you. Hope you're having fun, please reach out when you can. I miss you, too!

I add about a dozen red heart emojis before I hit send.

"You're smiley all of a sudden," Mom says with a smirk. "Good news from a friend?"

I grin. "Serenity's coming home soon. I can't wait to see her."

"Well," Dad pipes up. "I hope you'll see her even sooner than you think."

And now we're aboard the Edmonds–Kingston ferry. Our car is parked in the ship's underbelly, and we are standing near the front of the boat, in the briny marine air. Mom and I are here together, leaning against the green railing while Dad gets coffee and snacks from the indoor cafeteria. We are still docked at the beach in Edmonds, waiting for the full load of passengers. The ferry will take us across the Puget Sound to the town of Kingston.

Serenity hasn't texted me back since that one message. But now I'm pretty sure that's either because she lost service, or her phone is dead.

I reach out and touch the green rail, running my thumb across a ridged section where the paint is chipped and flaking. Short, choppy waves slap against the bottom of the ship. A seagull is perched on a wooden beam protruding from the water. The sea expands before us, bright and rippling and blue.

Dad comes up behind us. "So they didn't have a huge braces-friendly selection," he says. He's holding a tray with two coffees in paper cups, plus a small brown bag. "But I got you a chocolate chip cookie. Hopefully that'll do."

Chocolate chip cookies are always fine by me. I shove my hand inside the crinkly paper bag. Draw it out, take a huge bite.

The ferry blasts its horn. I jump and cover my ears. There's a slight jolt underfoot as we begin our forward momentum. Our journey across the water.

Mom says, "Why don't we go for a walk around the deck?"

I nod my agreement. We move toward the back of the boat while I eat my cookie. When we reach the end, I look out at the distance between us and the mainland. The ship creates a long, wide wake. It reminds me of a shimmery trail left by a fat slug.

Dad taps my shoulder and points. "Look," he says. "A jellyfish."

I follow his gaze, and sure enough, there's a jellyfish. A milky, transparent blob floating near the surface of the water.

We fall into a peaceful silence for a few minutes. Only us and the wind and the waves.

Then Mom clears her throat and says, "So. Where was I?"

"You told me about your friend in high school, who wanted to grow his hair long, but couldn't because of his parents."

"Right. And we were saving the rest to share with your dad, because he was a big part of it. I'm back on track now.

"For years, I really wanted to know what it meant to be Native. I wanted to reconnect with my culture, and learn the truth about my family and heritage. This lasted from my adolescence into adulthood. But I didn't do anything about it until I met your father. I was twenty-one, he was twenty-two. Your father was a student at the UW, and I was working at a coffeeshop a few blocks off campus."

"It's true," Dad says. "I charmed her with my good looks and impressed her with my massive textbooks."

I sigh. "Yeah, yeah. I've heard about the coffeeshop a thousand times already."

Mom smiles. "Anyways, we started dating in the summer of 1998. And your father took me out to the Seafair Powwow in Discovery Park."

Their gazes meet, and both of my parents seem to soften. They're still so in love, it actually disgusts me sometimes.

"I'd never been to a powwow before," she says. "But he didn't know that. We were still just getting to know each other. And although he knew I was Native American, he didn't know much about the adoption, or my general disconnection from the culture. So as we were walking around, admiring the dancers and the regalia, he kept asking me questions I didn't have answers to."

"I remember you were so embarrassed," Dad murmurs. "As if it was your own fault. As if you were a failure somehow, just because you didn't know what it meant to smudge."

"Donnie, that's *exactly* how it felt! I was on a date with a bright, interesting young college student. A guy with goals and ambitions and intimidating textbooks. And who was I? The girl from the coffeeshop, with zero interest in pursuing a degree in higher education. At that point in my life, most people only found me interesting *because* I was Native, and yet, I knew nothing about *being* Native. I was so afraid of disappointing you."

Dad clasps her arm in a movement so swift, it startles me. He keeps his grip on her elbow with one hand and reaches for her face with the other. He sweeps a stray lock of hair back from her forehead. Cups her cheek with his palm.

"You have never disappointed me," he says. "Not once, in all these years."

Her throat bobs as she swallows. She places a gentle hand over his and says, "Same goes for you."

Now Dad is leaning in to kiss her forehead, and I look away all awkwardly, pretending to inspect the bottom of my shoe.

As they pull apart, Mom says, "Okay. The ferry is docking soon. No more distractions.

"While we were at the powwow, I basically ended up telling your father my life story. I told him the same anecdotes I told you today, with the bullies and Uncle Phil, and Todd and his hair. I told your father about all the questions and yearnings that had been growing within me for years. And he listened and asked me, 'Why don't we try to find them?' I said, 'Try to find who?' He was like, 'Your parents.'

"We discussed it a little bit between ourselves, but your father was the one who handled most of the investigative work. It seemed like the sort of mystery that should have taken years to solve, but two days after the Seafair Powwow, your dad came into the coffeeshop and said, 'I think I found your family.' I didn't believe him at first. I thought he was pulling my chain. But he insisted, 'I mean it. I have a surname and an address in Indianola. We can go this Saturday, if you have the day off from work.'"

With a start, I realize the bag my cookie came in is now crumpled in my fist. I realize my heart is pounding inside my chest.

I ask them, "And so you found Edith Graham?"

Dad tells me, "Actually, we met her brother."

Mom places her hand on my shoulder. "And we'll take you there, very soon. But first, we want to show you an important park."

27.

OLD MAN HOUSE

July 12

We reach the shoreline.

Boulders line the beach in a gradient scale: the rocks along the bottom are coated in algae and barnacles, the middle rows are dark and slick with seawater, and those along the top are dry and streaked with bird poop. The town of Kingston is straight ahead, and thickets of evergreen trees stand guard in every direction.

Inside the ferry's underbelly, the cars rev their engines and roll forward. We follow the flow of traffic down the ramp, and upstream through Kingston.

And along the way, Mom tells me about the park we're going to, which is also the historic site of a winter village called Old Man House. The place where Chief Seattle himself lived and died. She describes how hundreds of people lived together in that single structure. How this long-house dated back hundreds of years, while the gathering site at this village dated back thousands of years.

I listen to her voice and watch outside the window as we drive. There are long, yellowed grasses along the roadside. Walls of evergreen trees fall and rise, breaking open to reveal wide meadows. Horses stand around, their tails swishing. Bill-boards advertise lots for sale, where blackberry bushes and shrubs run wild.

Mom tells me about how long the Old Man House lasted. And she tells me about how the government burned it to the ground.

We arrive at the park—a waterfront park with benches, leafy green trees, and round concrete garbage bins. The small parking lot is positioned at the top of a slight hill. The rolling grass slants down toward the shore. The water here is calm and clear, like blue glass. No wind or boats disturb it; the whole area is peaceful, quiet.

Our car doors slam shut, one after another. I step forward, to stand beside my mother.

"This is it?"

"This is it."

My parents lead me down to the beach. Bainbridge Island is directly across the Agate Passage. Its land slopes upward, along the rise of a hill, covered in dense clusters of evergreen trees. I catch glimpses of modern-looking mansions tucked within the forest: the reflective glint of a window, the edge of a smooth wall.

The waterfront park is only an acre long. Mom said that Old Man House was much bigger, when it existed here.

"It's so pretty," I say as we reach the beach. The sand is wet and flat and dense. I leave neat, shallow footprints as I walk across it. I glance around, trying to imagine what Old Man House must have looked like.

I walk closer to the water, the thin stretch of beach that is littered with crumpled seaweed and broken seashells. I kneel and pick up a seashell fragment. It's white and ridged on one side, shiny and pearly pink on the other. It has a chipped corner, and I like that; it gives this little shell some personality. The next one I grab is swirled and pointy, like the top part of soft-serve ice cream.

"I brought this for you, if you want it."

I turn toward Mom's voice—she's standing behind me, holding my drawing pad.

"I've noticed you haven't been drawing as much these past few days," she says. "But I thought you might want to, while we're here. We'll go to our next destination soon, but we're just . . . waiting for something. A special surprise for you."

My heart stills. My fingers tingle, suddenly, with the urge to draw.

"Okay. Thank you."

I take the drawing pad to a bench. Mom follows and gives me my drawing pencil. I flip through the pages, fanning them out like I would with a flipbook. There are sketches of the view from Golden Gardens. Outlines of the flowers from my mother's garden. And the dog from the reservation: its happy, furry face; its shaggy little body; its wagging tail.

Finally, I find the next open page and run my fingertips against the textured ivory paper.

Then I press the tip of my pencil to it.

I sketch this scene in faint, careful lines. The shoreline, the water, the trees. Each flick of my wrist is met with a hushed whisper against the paper. The landscape materializes, one caress at a time. Shades of gray and swipes of line.

As it comes together, I add the outline of a building—a long, rectangular structure set on the sand. I'm not really sure what the Old Man House looked like in real life, but I'm improvising. I draw it in long, straight strokes, like cedar planks across a giant log cabin.

Mom leans close, peeking over my shoulder. "Beautiful," she says. "But it's missing something, don't you think?"

From my other shoulder, Dad says, "It's missing two things, actually."

I squint at the page. "What?"

"The dog," Dad tells me. "I miss your little dog. Draw it in, please."

The request makes me giggle. I sketch the woolly form into the corner of the page, near the shoreline. I give his ears some perk, like he's listening for something. The tail needs motion lines, obviously. And I draw a few paw prints behind it, to show where the dog came from.

Dad nods. "Perfect."

"Thanks. What else is missing?"

"The people."

My grip tightens on the pencil.

"Don't worry," Mom coos. "It's a common mistake. Landscape artists have been getting it wrong for years, for *generations*. But the American West has never been an empty wilderness. It has always had people and architecture, civilizations and traditions. If you want to draw these landscapes, Edie, please do it right by recognizing how full they are. Find the beauty others have missed, and show it the way only someone like *you* can."

I stare at the page, unsure of myself, unsure of my ability to do this.

"I'm not very good at illustrating people."

Mom and Dad both exchange glances and shrug, as if this isn't such a big deal.

"No offense, sweetie," Dad says. "But once upon a time, you weren't very good at drawing dogs or landscapes, either."

I laugh, harder and louder than I mean to. "Wow. Thanks."

"Honestly. But look at you *now*. You're so

talented. I'm amazed by how perfectly you captured this landscape, how easily you envisioned a
building you've never seen before. And the dog! I
mean, despite being drawn in pencil, this is one of
the most realistic pups I've ever seen."

"It's true," Mom agrees. "A few years back, you
made pretty typical kid drawings. And I've loved
and saved many of them, but when you were drawing suns wearing sunglasses and super-triangular
mountains, we didn't think you'd go on to make
the things you're creating now. It's been such an
amazing process, watching you learn and grow
and become the artist you are today."

"And you're still so young, Edie. You have so
much growth ahead of you."

"That's right. Practice makes perfect. Go ahead,
try it."

I take in a deep breath. Press the tip of my pencil to the paper.

The first few lines I draw are too awkward, too
hard. I erase and start over, erase and start over.
I imagine people in my mind and try to imagine
what they would've looked like, what they would've
been doing. I draw some inspiration from beaches
I've gone to before and imagine a setting not too

different from Golden Gardens. I draw a group of small children chasing one another, playing tag. I draw adults standing in circles, talking and gesturing with their hands. I draw someone skipping rocks across the water. I draw another person next to the dog, with a stick in their hand so they can play fetch together.

It's not perfect. But it's a start.

28.

PLEASE, COME IN

July 12

Before we left the house, my parents packed a picnic basket for us. We're digging into it here at the beach, and I'm shocked both by how hungry I am and by how painless it is to eat.

"My teeth feel okay right now," I announce proudly.

Mom grins. "Glad to hear it, sweetie."

We're eating smoked salmon, cheddar cheese, and crackers. We also have grapes and applesauce.

"Tell me what happened next. After Dad found the address in Indianola."

Mom's mouth is full, so she gestures for Dad to pick up where she left off.

"So we took the Edmonds–Kingston ferry, and I remember I was the one driving. I had a 1990 BMW M3, at the time. Cherry-red with custom wheels and a leather interior. That was the first car I ever owned that had automatic windows. God, that was a great vehicle. Her name was Jasmine, in case you were wondering. But I usually called her Jazzy."

Mom rolls her eyes so hard, I see nothing but whites for a second.

"Anyways, I thought Jazzy was pretty impressive. And I was trying really hard to impress your mom by taking her to that house in Indianola. I was also nervous, of course, because we had no idea what we'd find once we got there. We didn't know if anyone would still be living there. We didn't know if they'd welcome us. It was a big risk. But I was determined to see it through for your mom, so she wouldn't spend the rest of her life wondering, 'What if?'

"There was just one problem, with me trying to be impressive. Because our little road trip happened pre-GPS, and I sucked at reading paper maps. I'm probably the worst navigator in history. That's not an exaggeration."

Mom and I are starting to giggle.

"I'm serious! It was awful. We kept getting lost and having to turn around, and it was especially embarrassing, because there weren't *that* many roads out here back then. It was a pretty straight shot to our destination, and I managed to muck it up. And the entire time, I was thinking, 'Oh Lord. She'll never go on a date with me again, because now she knows I'm an idiot.'"

Mom gasps. "You're no such thing."

Dad shrugs. Smirks. "But that's exactly how it felt. I was dating a beautiful, interesting young woman who had put her trust in me. And I was terrified I wouldn't get it right for her."

She gapes at him. "*You*—"

"*Anyways*," Dad says. "I eventually realized I was reading the map upside down, hence the problem. And once I turned it around, finding the address didn't seem so difficult.

"We came to a long gravel driveway. There were some big trees on the property, and the house was right on the waterfront. It was a beautiful little cottage. It looked like something out of a storybook. I parked the car on the street and took your mother's hand. As we walked down the sloping driveway, I noticed she was shivering.

"We walked up to the porch. It was the summertime, remember, so the windows were cracked open. There was a screen door in front, and we could see through it. I remember the cabin's interior was shadowy, but in the background I could see a rocking chair. And a pile of blankets on top of an ottoman.

"I rang the doorbell. Your mother and I could hear it buzzing clearly, from where we were standing. We stood and waited, but it seemed like no one was coming. I reached out and knocked on the corner of the screen door. Still nothing.

"Your mother tugged on my hand and said, 'We tried, Donnie. No one's here. Let's go home.' And I said, 'No way. The windows are open and there's a truck parked on the side of the house. They probably just can't hear us.' Mom told me, 'Thank you for bringing me here. You have no idea how much it means to me. But this might be a mistake. We should go.'

"I rang the doorbell a second time. We'd come so far, and I hated the idea of turning back without at least talking to someone. And just as we were about to give up, a man stepped into view inside the house. With the shadows, neither of us could see his face, but it was clear from his size and stature that this was a man. A very large, strong-looking man.

"I grinned and tried my best to be charming. I said, 'Hello, sir. My name is Don Green, and this is my girlfriend, Lisa Miller. We're sorry to intrude like this, but we have a few questions for the family of this house. If it's not too much to ask.'

"He stared at us in silence, for what felt like whole minutes. It was a little unnerving, considering how we couldn't see his face while he looked back at us. But we held our ground, and I held your mother's hand. We endured the inspection.

"And then he came forward. His footsteps were slow and heavy. When he reached the screen door, we could finally see his face. Despite the differences in age and gender, the familial resemblance was absolutely striking. I remember your mother gasped at that first glimpse of him. He was tall and broad, and there were crow's feet around his eyes, laugh lines around his mouth. His salt-and-pepper hair was long and framed his face in two braids.

206

His brown eyes were wet and rimmed in red. He was on the verge of tears.

"We were all speechless, I think. No one said anything as he opened the screen door, stepped out onto the porch, and pulled your mother into a fierce hug. I remember your mother's shoulders shook as she held him. I remember his face crumpled as he dropped his chin to the top of her head. I remember he croaked the words 'I know who you are. I know who you are. It's you. You found your way home. You came back to us.' Tears streaked down his face, and he didn't bother to wipe them away.

"When they finally stepped apart, he shook my hand and held the screen door open for us. He said, 'My name is Theodore Graham. Please, come in.'"

29.

THE NECESSARY SMALL TALK

July 12

Mom is crying. Her eyes are glistening, her cheeks are shiny. I can tell she's trying not to sob from the little hiccuping sounds she's making.

I feel like crying, too, but I manage to hold it in. I reach my arms around her, holding her tight as we sit together on the park bench. Dad reaches around us both, making it a group hug.

The three of us sit like this for a while, listening to the birds chatter in the trees and watching the gentle waves lap against the shore. We wait for Mom to regain her composure. We wait until she says, "All right. I'm ready. Are you?"

I hesitate. "I just have one question."

"What's that, sweetie?"

"Am I—about to meet them?" I ask. "Are Theo and Edith still here?"

"Oh, Edie. If they were, you would've grown up with them."

I swallow the lump in my throat and nod several times, to show that I understand. To prove that I'm ready. When my parents agreed to open up with the truth, I kind of figured this would be it. That their stories would come to an end.

Where am I from?

After all this time, I'm finally going to learn the truth.

I just hope my heart won't shatter when I do.

Dad drives us to the address. The cabin is small and made of cedar planks. Built right on the waterfront, just as my dad described it.

There's a truck parked out front. I wasn't expecting anyone else to be here, and I shoot my parents questioning looks. "Are you sure we're in the right place?"

Mom smiles. "Of course. Don't you recognize that truck?"

I glance at it again. I guess it does look vaguely

familiar, but I'm not sure where I've seen it before.

I'm controlling my breathing and bracing myself for anything as we walk up the porch, to the front door. It must be the same screen door my parents looked through, because the metal frame looks old, and the screen is gauzy and shadowy.

Dad pushes the screen door open. Mom calls out, "We're here!"

And the most unexpected person of all comes flying toward me, her arms flailing as she shrieks, "SURPRISE!"

Serenity crashes into me with a bone-crushing hug.

I'm so amazed, I scream in her ear as I squeeze her back.

She winces and laughs and keeps embracing me. This is one of the best hugs of my entire life.

"What are you doing here?"

"Your dad called my dad this morning, when we finally got service back. He said something about a family emergency? Then your uncle Phil came and picked me up, and here we are."

I can't believe this. I pull back to look her in the eyes. I glimpse Uncle Phil behind her, and he gives me a nod and a little wave. Serenity grips my shoulders, returning my attention to her.

"I'm sorry I didn't really respond to your texts today," she says sheepishly. "I lied, I did have service at that point. But I was supposed to surprise you, so I couldn't really *say* that, you know?"

"It's okay," I tell her. "I'm just so happy to see you." I give her another hug and turn my head to meet my mother's gaze. "You're okay with her being here?"

Mom shrugs. "I meant it when I said no more secrets. Besides, your uncle Phil called me after breakfast this morning and convinced me it would be a good idea to bring her. To give you a happy surprise."

"That's right," Uncle Phil says. "We needed to lighten the mood around here. And during the ferry ride, I got to tell Serenity all about how to care for a pet duck. Since I'm the expert in that field."

Serenity nods. "It's true. I want one."

"I also brought my portable generator over and showed her how to set that up. So we have power in the house now; you're welcome. And, uh, kiddo." Uncle Phil gestures at himself. "Just wondering, where's my hug?"

I giggle and run across the room and launch myself into his open arms.

While we're hugging, a thought crosses my

mind. "Uncle Phil," I say. "Did you try to convince Mom to have you bring Amelia, too?"

Uncle Phil releases me. Scratches the back of his neck. "I considered it," he tells me. "But once I picked Serenity up, and she told me about some recent drama—I'm glad I only recommended one of your best friends."

I hold his gaze and absorb his words while Mom gasps softly behind me.

"What drama?" she asks. "Is everything okay?"

"Yes," I whisper. "I just don't—I'm not sure if Amelia and I are friends anymore. If we'll ever be friends again."

Uncle Phil places a protective hand on my shoulder. Mom swallows, her gaze dropping to her hands.

Dad's voice is solemn. "I'm sorry to hear that, sweetie."

Serenity steps forward. "I'm sorry, too. But I'm not surprised. Amelia hasn't been a good friend to either of us for a long time now. I only still hung out with her because you wanted to."

"I always thought it would be the three of us," I tell her. "Together forever."

"I used to believe that, too. But friendships only

work if everyone remains kind to each other. Amelia used to be one of the nicest people I knew." Her shoulders deflate. She shakes her head sadly. "Not anymore."

"Well. As sad as it is, I'm glad I can still count on you."

I turn to my parents, curious and ready to change the subject.

"So," I say. "This is where you met Theo."

Mom nods. "Yes. This room hasn't changed much."

I look around, taking in the sofas stacked with wilted cushions, the creaky hardwood floors, the dust particles swirling in the sunlight. A canoe paddle is mounted on the wall above the window. Albums line a shelf above an old record player. An ancient television set stands in the corner of the room. The tiny box has silver antenna rods, and its curved screen is framed by a wood-grain border, with two chrome dials and a teeny-tiny built-in speaker.

It occurs to me that this is probably where Edith Graham watched TV and movies. This might be how she saw Sacheen Littlefeather's speech and decided to take a chance on her own dreams.

"Is this—?"

She nods, confirming my suspicions. "Yes. They both grew up here, and this was her television set. When Edith got her first job, Theo said she went out and spent her entire first paycheck on this thing." Mom gives a breathy laugh. Crosses the room. "He said she was always impulsive like that, and she always loved movies. She grew up watching everything in black and white, because their mother refused to splurge on a color TV."

She presses the power button, and the television hums to life in a blur of static. The screen turns solid blue, while the word "PLAY" flashes in the top left corner, in pixelated white letters. Mom clicks the button again, and it goes back to black with a gentle zapping sound.

"I can't imagine watching full movies on that," I murmur.

Mom gives a shrug. "Times have changed. Now," she says, "are you ready to hear the rest of the story?"

I nod and take a seat on the sofa. Serenity and Uncle Phil settle in on either side of me. Mom and Dad go to the love seat directly across from us.

And she draws her breath to begin.

30.

WHAT MOM TELLS ME

When we came inside this cabin for the first time, Theo sat us down in the living room, just like this. We chatted for hours, sharing stories, getting to know each other. He had so many questions about where I'd been and what I'd gone through since the adoption. I was open and honest, because there was something about him that made me feel safe. We had this immediate connection, and he was my uncle, my family. I knew I could trust him.

He taught me our family's history. He said that his parents—my grandparents—were married in

1945. My grandfather served in the military, as an infantryman in the US Army. He died in combat in the Korean War in 1952. Theo's memories of his father were few and vague, because he was born in 1948, and his father enlisted in 1951. Edith was born on February 28, 1952; she never met her father at all.

To support the household, my grandmother worked as a maid at a country club in Kingston. She also took on various domestic service jobs from some of the club's members. She worked long hours and didn't make much money, but she made sure her children had food on the table every night.

When Theo was a teenager, he got a job at the local five-and-dime store. He worked in that same store his entire life, and he always lived in this same house. Throughout his life, he was a passionate activist, and he participated in some major demonstrations for Native rights. He never married or had children of his own, but he loved his family more than anything. When his mother became ill in the mid-1970s and had to stop working, he took good care of her. And he continued to look after her until she passed in 1985.

As I'm sure you've learned, Edith—my mother—

worked at the ferry docks, before shocking her family with her grand plan to move to Los Angeles. She wanted to become a professional actress.

Theo said that he and his mother didn't disapprove of her plans, but . . . they were afraid for her. Their life here in Suquamish might not have been perfect, but it was consistent. They knew what to expect from this place. They knew how to survive in this place. The same couldn't be said for LA. And Edith was young and idealistic, maybe a little naive. They loved her very much and didn't want to see her get crushed.

But of course, they still let her go. She was determined, and neither of them could deny her anything.

Ultimately, her acting career didn't work out. She came home in the winter of 1977, a few weeks before her twenty-fifth birthday. She didn't return to work at the ferry docks, because she wanted to be a stay-at-home mother. My grandmother and Uncle Theo agreed to provide for her and help her raise me.

Edith planned to give birth here, with the assistance of a midwife. If that had happened, it's very possible I never would've been taken to an orphanage.

Every week or two, Theo traveled to Seattle to complete various errands. Remember, this was in the era before smartphones and the internet. You couldn't order stuff online, couldn't pay bills online. There are certain chores adults need to do, and back then, they needed to do those things in person. And at that point, the town of Indianola didn't have access to a lot of that stuff. Which is why Theo needed to travel to the mainland.

It was August, and Edith was far along in her pregnancy. Most days, she was extremely uncomfortable, and spent her time knitting baby clothes down by the waterfront. She'd made all kinds of onesies and booties and hats. She hoped the clothes would fit me and keep me warm in the coming fall and winter.

When Theo told her he was going to Seattle, she perked up and set aside her knitting needles. She said, "Can I come with you this time?" He eyed her belly and said, "I'm not sure if that's a great idea." She said, "I really feel much better today. And I want to go to Pike Place Market. I'd love to have some fresh flowers in the house, and I'm starting to run low on yarn. Take me with you on your errands. Please, Theo."

Naturally, he took her. And he would regret it for the rest of his life.

The day started out fine. They took the ferry to Seattle. They went to Pike Place Market. Edith picked out a bouquet of wildflowers. She chose a variety of yarns in colors that reminded her of autumn leaves: warm reds and blazing oranges and golden yellows.

They took their time and went to grab some lunch. Theo brought her over to a picnic table, so she could sit and relax while he ordered their food. Edith was in high spirits, and still insisted she felt fine, but the physical exertion was starting to wear on her.

When Theo brought their food back to the table, the situation had changed dramatically. She was seated with her back turned to the table, because her belly stood out too far for her to face it. And she was no longer smiling, no longer cheery. Both of her hands were clutched to her lower abdomen, and her teeth were gritted in pain.

Theo remembered telling her, "We need to get you back on the ferry. We need to leave right now." She was clearly in labor, and they had to bring her back to the midwife, to the safety of their own home.

"Just give me a minute," she said. "Give me a minute, and I'll catch my breath."

Their lunch sat untouched on the table. The steaming food grew cold. A few bold crows flocked near, cawing at their backs.

Finally, Edith rose shakily to her feet. Theo held her hand as they moved away from the table. But she stopped and exclaimed, "The yarns! Don't forget the yarns." He grabbed the shopping bag, but left the wildflowers and the food containers behind.

People stared as they hobbled along. Theo's car was parked under the viaduct. They had to make it back to his car and drive a short distance down the pier to secure a spot on the ferry for Bainbridge Island. Then they'd have to drive the ten miles from that port to their house in Indianola.

As they backtracked through Pike Place Market, Edith was hit by another wave of contractions. She cried out and her knees buckled. She nearly crumpled to the ground, but Theo held her up. He said, "We need to keep going, little sister. I'm sorry, I'm so sorry. Please forgive me, but we can't stay here."

A shopkeeper came forward and suggested that they go to the hospital. He offered to call an ambulance.

Theo told him, "We appreciate your concern, but we're almost home. Thank you."

Edith's breathing was shallow and pained, but she wordlessly nudged her brother forward. They tried to continue on their way.

The shopkeeper called out, "Are you sure you don't want me to call an ambulance?"

Theo replied, "We're okay."

Together, they walked as quickly as they could. They made it to the street where his car was parked. There were only a few blocks left to go when they heard the low wail of sirens.

The shopkeeper had called an ambulance. And it was about to find them.

When Theo got to this part of the story, he told me he was on the verge of howling. That's the exact word he used, howl. *He said he wanted to cry and scream and sob all at once.*

Edith must've known, because she placed a gentle hand on his cheek. She told him, "It's okay, Theo. Breathe. Everything will be okay."

Theo didn't understand how she could believe in luck. But if she could find the strength to get help in that moment, to put herself in such a vulnerable position—once again, he couldn't deny her. All he could do was stand by and support her.

So they stopped. They waited for the ambulance. When it turned the corner, he waved them down. Sure enough, the paramedics confirmed they'd received a call from someone at Pike Place, who'd witnessed "a pregnant Indian woman in need of immediate assistance."

They admitted her to the hospital. And she endured eight hours of labor before I came.

Theo said that I made them both believe in love at first sight.

He said they both cried when they saw me cradled in the doctor's arms. The umbilical cord hadn't been cut yet. My eyes were squeezed shut and my hands were balled into fists. Theo claimed that I looked like a tiny boxer. Like I entered this world already braced for a fight.

Edith was still weak and gasping from the labor. But her eyes shone with pride and she said, "My baby. My baby. Look at you. I love you already."

Then the doctor snipped the umbilical cord. He handed me off to a nurse, who darted out of the room without a backward glance.

And that was it.

31.

WHAT HAPPENED NEXT

Edith tried to sit up in the hospital bed. She asked, "Where are you taking her?"

The doctor waved her concerns off. "We just have a few routine tests to run. To make sure the infant is in a stable condition."

"Can't I hold her first?"

"It should only be a moment, ma'am."

The doctor excused himself from the room, and Theo and Edith waited to see what would happen in tense, emotional silence.

It wasn't a moment. It was an hour.

A knock sounded at the door, and a man walked in. He was dressed in a black suit, with a binder tucked under his arm.

He introduced himself as a social worker.

He had some questions to ask about their living situation.

He opened his binder; it contained multiple documents and a legal pad.

The first thing he wanted to verify was Edith's marital status. He noted the use of her maiden name when she was admitted to the hospital, and the absence of any rings on her fingers.

Edith held her head high. "It's true. I'm an unmarried woman."

He scribbled a note into his legal pad.

The next thing he wanted to verify was Theo's identity. He asked if he was, in fact, the same Theodore Graham who had been arrested during the protests at Fort Lawton.

Theo said nothing.

The man tapped his pen against the legal pad, waiting.

Then he whisked a court document out of his folder and read it aloud. He recited charges placed against Theo at the time of his arrest, along with the physical descriptions and information available about him.

Feeling pressured, Theo admitted the truth. "Yes. I'm the same Theodore Graham."

The man pursed his lips and scribbled another note.

Next, he asked how many people lived in their house.

Edith answered, "Three adults."

Who was the third adult?

"Our mother."

The questions continued. The social worker wanted to know how old their mother was. He wanted to know what their combined family income was. He wanted to know who completed what chores around the house. He wanted to know who the baby's father was. When Edith told him about that, he wanted to know why she was in California. When she explained the dreams and goals she'd worked toward as a younger woman, he listened with no reaction whatsoever.

Throughout the interrogation, Theo and Edith tried to remain strong and sweet and open. They tried to make a good impression. Edith smiled frequently, even though her lips quivered.

Finally, the social worker clicked his pen and looked up. His expression was perfectly blank.

"I believe that's everything I need to know," he

said. *"Thank you for your time."*

He closed the binder and rose from the chair. Theo and Edith exchanged looks of panic.

Before he reached the door, she cried out, *"Please. Please, can I see my child now?"*

He paused with his hand on the doorknob. *"I'm not sure that will be possible, Miss Graham."*

"Oh no. Please, sir, I—" Her eyes shone bright with tears. Her chest heaved with small, quick breaths. *"I know we don't seem like much. I know what you're probably thinking. We're not exactly conventional or perfect, but this is—this is the role I'm meant to have. I'm supposed to be a mother. I can promise you, she will be loved. She will be loved so fiercely. Please understand me. I will keep her safe and happy."*

He stood with his back turned to them. And for a single, airless moment, Edith thought she'd gotten through to him. She thought he wasn't about to do the terrible thing other Native women had warned her about.

But he simply responded, *"I will pray for you, child."*

And he left.

32.

SPLIT-FEATHER SYNDROME

July 12

Her final words hover in the air.

"What do you mean, 'he left'?" I glance back and forth between my parents. The air grows heavy, difficult to breathe. "Did the doctor bring you back? Was everything okay?"

"The doctor had no intention of bringing me back to her, Edie."

"But she was your mother. She loved you. She wanted you back. They couldn't just—they couldn't keep you away from her. That makes no sense. H-how could they do something like that?"

"Because my mother was an unmarried woman, who was flighty and irresponsible, since she got pregnant while she was off chasing unrealistic dreams in California. Because my uncle was a convicted criminal, who was political and radical and possibly violent, since he dared to take a stand as a Native activist. Because the third adult in their house was an ailing old woman, who couldn't be expected to care for a newborn baby, despite successfully raising two children on her own and working in domestic service her entire life.

"That was how the social worker analyzed their situation. He added up the facts of their life story and concluded that my family was unfit to care for me. He didn't think they should be allowed to keep me. And so, no one brought me back to my mother's delivery room. I was taken away from the hospital and sent to an orphanage. That was where I stayed, until Grandma and Grandpa Miller came and found me."

I'm shaking my head. "No. No, that can't be real. That couldn't have happened."

"I'm sorry, Edie." Her voice cracks. "But it's the truth. They took me away. And my mother never saw me again."

Serenity grasps my hand in both of hers. She

rubs her thumb back and forth across my skin. Uncle Phil places a gentle palm against the center of my back.

Mom says, "For many years, Native children were forcibly removed from their families and communities."

I'm still shaking my head. Too shocked to do anything else.

"This is why my mother didn't want to give birth in a hospital. This is why she and my uncle tried so hard to avoid it, even when she began going into labor in downtown Seattle. They knew that state child welfare and private adoption agencies were actively seeking out Native children. They knew of friends and neighbors and distant relatives whose kids were taken."

Serenity gives my hand another squeeze. I can hear Uncle Phil's breath catch in his chest. I can feel Dad watching my reactions closely.

Mom licks her lips and says, "Between the 1940s and 1970s, about one-third of Native children were separated from their families. Until Congress passed the Indian Child Welfare Act in 1978."

I somehow find my voice again. "*Congress* got involved?"

She nods. "Took them long enough, if you ask

me. But at the same time, I'm grateful, because when I had you—" She's still nodding, her head bobbing in a frantic motion that seems a little out of her control. "My God, if anything had happened to you—"

Dad wraps his arms around her, hugging her against his side. She tucks her chin and curls into his embrace. "Nothing ever did," he says softly. "Nothing ever will."

My heart is heavy as a stone inside my chest.

So this is what happened to my mother and grandmother. I imagined so many different scenarios on our way here, and I thought for sure I'd prepared myself. I thought I was ready and braced for the worst.

But I didn't picture this.

I wasn't ready for something this cruel.

I wasn't ready for this horrific injustice.

I'm up and off the couch, striding across the room to my parents, throwing my arms around them. Until today, I didn't realize what a beautiful and wonderful gift this is. The right to hug your loved ones, whenever you want to.

I will never take these hugs for granted again.

33.

DIRECTLY ACROSS THE SEA

July 12

A few moments later, Dad presses a quick kiss to my forehead. He looks me in the eye and asks, "Are you all right?"

I nod.

"We brought some salmon and salad supplies for dinner. Your mother and I figured we should all eat here tonight. You can explore the cabin, plan for the film with Serenity. Maybe even get some drawing time in. Okay?"

"Okay."

"I'd offer to help with dinner," Uncle Phil says,

"but I only know how to grill burgers. I'm useless at cooking anything else." He sighs, like this is a huge regret in his life. Then an idea occurs to him. His mood brightens. "Unless you brought some cereal? I pour a mean bowl of cereal."

Again with the dumb jokes.

Mom narrows her eyes at him. Dad's eyebrows shoot straight up. Serenity peeks at him with an unimpressed look on her face.

They're all giving him these stares, because this *clearly* isn't the time for stupid jokes.

But since this is Uncle Phil, I can't help myself.

I snort. It comes out loud and weird. And then I giggle, because I snorted so loud, and that giggle turns into a restrained laugh.

"What?" Uncle Phil asks, his voice sincere, eyes twinkling with mischief. "It's all about the milk-to-cereal ratio. If you go too heavy with the cereal, it dries out fast. If you go too heavy with milk, everything falls into chaos. It's a fine art, Edie. A balance, if you will."

"Uncle Phil. No one eats cereal for dinner."

"What are you talking about? That's my life at least three or four days of the week."

Serenity says, "Then why don't you learn how to cook?"

Uncle Phil gives a long-suffering sigh. "Because what's the point, when I live in an era of fast food drive-throughs and instant noodle cups?"

And somehow, I'm still laughing. Even while my heart feels like it's covered in bruises.

"You could still help," Dad says. "Everything is prepped and prewashed, since we don't have running water. All we need to do is grill the salmon and potatoes, set out some utensils."

"Fine, Donnie. Twist my arm."

Serenity perks up. "I can help, too!"

As the three of them go to the kitchen, Mom chuckles and tucks a lock of hair behind my ear. She rises from her seat. "Come outside with me," she says. "I want to show you something."

I follow her outside, and we walk together along the water's edge. The air is warm and breezy. We've both removed our shoes, and the shoreline is cool and coarse.

"Our time together was limited," Mom says. "But I'm so grateful I got to know Uncle Theo. I'm glad I came here when I did. I'm glad he was able to tell me our family's history."

The waves pull in and out, gentle as a hushed breath.

"He was diagnosed with cancer a couple years after we first met. He died on October 30, 2001; he was only fifty-three years old." She inhales shakily. "We scattered his ashes right here, in the waters of the Salish Sea, his home. It was what he wanted. And Edith's ashes were scattered here, too. She died suddenly at the age of forty, from a fatal arrhythmia."

I don't know what an arrhythmia is, and I can't bring myself to ask. So instead I say, "And he left you this house?"

"Yes. Your father and I have maintained this house over the years. It never felt like an option to sell it. And after we got married, he even asked if I wanted to move here, to live permanently on this side of the water. He thought I might want to raise our family in Indianola, rather than Seattle."

"*Really?* Why didn't you?"

Mom licks her lips. Shrugs. "It's hard to explain now. But I thought you'd have a better chance at a 'normal' childhood in the city." She shakes her head. "I think I was just afraid of how you'd react to this whole story. I was an adult when I learned everything, and it shook me to my very core. I wanted to protect you, as long as I could. I didn't want you to feel lost or confused or angry."

I breathe in deep; I understand where she's coming from now. I can see why she hid the box from me.

And she still hasn't told me everything. I'm aware of that. But all this sadness is so exhausting. I'm not sure either of us can take much more of it.

So I simply tell her, "Grandma Edith's head shots were really beautiful."

It works. She smiles. "Yes. They were."

"She looked like you."

"She looked a lot like you, too. You have her smile."

I press my fingers to my lips. "I guess I did. Probably not anymore, once my braces come off."

"Smiles aren't beautiful because of teeth. Smiles are beautiful because of a person's spirit." Mom moves behind me. She wraps her arms around my shoulders. And she says, "You have her spirit, Edie. That's something no one can ever change or take away."

I tilt my head. I hadn't thought of it that way before.

Mom lowers her head and whispers, "Do you see

that place? Directly across the sea?"

"Yes." The land across the water is unevenly sculpted. I follow the rise of a rugged, green landscape, dotted with houses and buildings that look so tiny from here, they're almost unnoticeable. Hazy blue mountains cut sharp lines into the periwinkle sky.

"Does it look familiar to you? This particular spot?"

I try squinting. The sea stretches before me, vast and bright and inviting. The air is salty, with a crisp aftertaste like a sip of iced water. Sailboats and speedboats leave foamy white trails in their wake. Two ferries are about to cross paths in the middle of their journey, their bloated white bodies lined with rows of tinted black windows. The sky curves overhead, like the interior of a great blue bowl. "Keep looking," she urges. "You know this place."

I scan the landscape. Blue water and green lands and distant mountains in every direction. To the south, just beyond the green hills, I realize a hint of downtown Seattle is visible. From here, the skyscrapers look like toy blocks propped up in the lowlands between hills.

The recognition dawns on me slowly. I do know this landscape. I do know this place.

I gently pull away from my mother's embrace, to look around at my surroundings. I breathe it all in. The sea and the sand. The evergreen trees and mountains. The rise and fall of this land.

And I gasp. "Mom," I say, "are we across from Golden Gardens?"

She laughs a little. Beams at me. "Yes, Edie," she says. "This is how close we are. How close we've always been. This is where we belong. You and me." Mom pulls me into another hug. I hug her back, arms squeezed around her middle.

My smile is a heartfelt, unstoppable thing.

34.

A SALMON GOING UPSTREAM

July 12

It's an hour before sunset when we sit around the outdoor table. The sky is orange and pink and brilliant. The evergreen trees around us look golden in the slanting light. The water shimmers and flashes. Our dinner consists of salmon and salad, with wild blackberries and roasted fingerling potatoes.

It looks and smells divine. And it tastes even better.

I'm pretty sure this is my first proper meal since I got braces. Every now and then, I take a bite that makes me flinch, but it's not too bad. Not nearly like it was a few days ago.

Uncle Phil and Serenity are sharing funny stories. Loud and laughing. Mom is lifting a forkful of potatoes, smiling as she bites. Covering her mouth when she giggles. Dad catches my eye from across the table; he cocks his head and gives me a discreet thumbs-up. I understand the question he's asking and respond with the warmest smile possible. He grins back and returns his attention to his food, happy to see me happy.

And then—a sound carries across the water. A pleasant hum, a building rhythm. I set my fork aside and turn to look over my shoulder.

"Guys," I say. "What *is* that?"

The table falls silent, as the sound—the *singing*—strengthens and rises. Waves lap against the shore, swelling with an incoming tide. And out there, in the middle of the sea, is a line of— *canoes*. Paddles plunging into the water in brisk, even swipes. Voices harmonizing and bellowing in a language I've never heard before.

I push away from the table. I rise from my chair.

The canoes keep coming and going. They are long, with pointed sterns and elaborately painted bodies. Some are wreathed in green cedar boughs. Others have flags hoisted in the air, waving in the wind.

"Are they—?" I leave the question unfinished, because I already know the answer. It's obvious.

They're all Natives. And they're all going—*somewhere*.

I take off running down the beach, jumping over shells and boulders and strands of kelp. At this point, at least a dozen canoes have gone by, and they aren't slowing down.

Where are they going?

As I stand at the edge of the shore, I catch glimpses of their flags, the words written across their canoes—some are written in another language, the same language they must be singing in. But there are tribal names, too—the Puyallup, the Quinault, the Cowichan.

An elderly woman in a cedar-woven hat sits at the front of one canoe, facing the paddlers. She's leading one of the songs as they go, and I watch as she checks over her shoulder and sees me. She cocks her head to the side and lifts one hand in a friendly wave, even though we don't know each other. Even though she's never seen me before.

I wave back, lifting my arm high, spreading my fingers wide.

"Edie!"

I spin around to find my mother behind me. Her smile is wide and carefree.

"What do you think, sweetie?" she asks. "Should we follow along?"

I nod, fast and insistent. "What's happening? What is this?"

And she says, "You'll see."

We drive back to the park where Old Man House once stood. The same park where dozens of canoes have now been pulled up along the shoreline.

It's the best kind of chaos. A landscape filled with songs and laughter and hugging family members. An evening of pink skies and bright smiles and splashing waters.

My family scatters. Uncle Phil starts chatting with a group of guys his age, while my parents introduce themselves to an elderly couple sitting in lawn chairs. Serenity and I take off on our own along the shore, observing everything, meeting gazes and waving hello to strangers. All the canoes have gathered here, each packed with visitors from all over—the Snoqualmie, the Cowlitz, the Swinomish.

Serenity tugs on my sleeve. "Edie," she says excitedly. "Are you thinking what I'm thinking?"

"What?"

She beams and says, "This is it. This is the story."

"For the film?" I turn the possibility over in my mind. Find myself nodding. "Yes," I say. "You're *right*. This is it. The perfect ending."

Near the end of the line, I glimpse a canoe from Tulalip. A group of boys about our age are skipping rocks across the water, shouting and boisterous.

One of them is wearing a backward-facing baseball cap, with a tuft of black hair sticking through the gap. His teeth are bright white in contrast against his skin, and he's laughing at something his friends have said. Another boy snaps at him, "Roger, come *on*."

"Okay, okay."

Roger turns around to grab more rocks, and I come to an abrupt stop. He sees me and straightens, eyes wide and blinking. His friends notice and follow his gaze, straight to me.

"Edie," Serenity says. "What are you—?"

"Hey!" Roger grins, his entire face brightening. "I *know* you."

I give a slightly awkward wave. "Hi," I say. Then I gesture at myself and add, "Edie." In case he forgot my name.

"I remember. It's good to see you again." He shows me his handful of rocks. "Wanna join us? We're in the middle of a competition. It's a lot more fun than it looks, I promise."

Serenity and I exchange glances, and a mutual, encouraging shrug. "Sure," I say. "Thanks."

And as the sun dips below the horizon, we send ripples across the water that never seem to end.

EPILOGUE

WHERE ARE YOU GOING?

August 28

"Haaappy birthday to you!"

Mom closes her eyes. Breathes in, focusing on her wish. Then she leans forward and blows the candles out.

We clap and cheer and scream for her. I launch out of my seat to throw my arms around her. She laughs as she clutches me back, and soon I feel Dad's arms around us both. We hold on tight for several seconds, before Uncle Phil groans.

"I love the love, but can we please try the cake now? Serenity and I need some sugar." He shoots her a conspiratorial glance. "Right?"

My best friend nods her agreement. "Definitely."

And that's when we finally release each other.

As Dad starts cutting the cake into slices, I run inside the cabin to retrieve my gift for Mom.

We've spent a lot of time here in Indianola over the summer. I love this place so much. I've loved learning more about my family, my culture. I've loved seeing the landscape, drawing it over and over from this perspective.

It would be easy to feel discouraged here, in the place Grandma Edith and Uncle Theo returned to after Mom was taken from them. It would be easy to let the sadness win, knowing they stayed here all those years later, hoping and waiting and wishing to see her again.

But I try to stay positive. I try to focus on the people I have, rather than those who are missing. I try to focus on the future ahead of us, rather than the past.

I grab the small, wrapped box for Mom, plus the handmade card to go along with it. And I hope— with every ounce of love in my heart—that she will be proud of what I made for her.

My phone vibrates in my pocket, and I pull it

out to check the message.

Roger: Tell your mom I say happy b-day! And good luck with the surprise presentation ☺

I text back, Thanks! Fingers crossed.

As I head back outside, Mom greets me with a wide grin. "Well, what do we have here?"

Serenity pipes up. "Open it and find out, Mrs. Green!"

Mom chuckles. "All right. The card goes first."

I plop back down in my chair and watch as she holds the front cover up for everyone to see. It's simple cursive, and reads, *Happy Birthday, Mom! I love you.*

"Very nice, Edie," Dad says, nodding his approval.

Mom turns the card around to face her again, and she gasps as she opens it.

"Oh, honey. It's amazing. I love it."

She holds the card open and shows the interior pages. It's a portrait-landscape drawing, featuring everyone around this table: Mom, Dad, Uncle Phil, Serenity, and me. In the drawing, we're standing together along the edge of the water, in front of the Indianola cabin. I colored the background in pretty shades of blue and green. And I really have gotten better at illustrating people. Everyone is clearly recognizable.

"I want my own version of that drawing," Uncle Phil declares. "I want an exact copy, so that I can hang it up beside my painting of William."

"We'll be sure to get you one," Mom promises.

As she turns her attention to her gift, Dad catches my gaze with a sly grin. Serenity gives my shoulder a nudge, and we exchange secret smiles, too. They both know what's inside the box. They're probably just as excited for her reaction as I am.

Mom opens the wrapping paper with a clean rip.

The box is tiny enough to fit in her palm. It has no labels, no markings to hint at what's inside. It looks to be about the size of a jewelry gift box.

She lifts the lid. Her eyes widen as she removes the little rectangular piece of paper.

Uncle Phil squints. "What is it, Lisa?"

She blinks. Gives a small, breathy laugh. Turns the paper around for him to see. "It's a movie ticket," she says. "To an exclusive preview of their short film. Tonight."

Serenity and I both start giggling, out of

nerves and excitement.

"I thought you said you weren't finished yet!" Mom cries. "The film festival is two days away, and you had me convinced!"

"The girls finished their work last week," Dad tells her. "And I finalized my video editing duties yesterday. We wanted to surprise you."

"It certainly worked. And it says here, the screening will happen 'immediately after cake'?"

"That's right," I say.

Mom flashes another grin. "Why wait? Let's eat our cake and watch the film, too."

Serenity and I erupt in cheers. My heart beats fast, a little frantic. I wonder what she'll think of it.

We each bring our slices of cake and scoops of ice cream inside. I sit on the couch, sandwiched between my parents. Uncle Phil takes the rocking chair in the corner. Serenity sits cross-legged on the floor in front of me.

Dad already has everything all set up. He exported the video onto a DVD, so all we need to do is turn the TV on, switch to HDMI-3, and hit play.

The film begins with the title in crisp white letters, over a black screen:

Bruno Goes Home

A short film by Edie Green and Serenity Jones

The title screen fades away.

Serenity's voice says, *"Once upon a time, there was a little dog named Bruno."*

As she speaks, my animation fades into focus. Bruno sits on his haunches, in the middle of a blurry, pencil-sketched marketplace. But despite the bustling crowd and Bruno's wagging tail, it's clear the dog is alone. No one comes to give Bruno pets or belly rubs. No one walks over to say hello.

"One day, Bruno lost his family in the middle of a crowded marketplace. He wandered around, in search of the people he belonged to. But they were nowhere to be found."

Her narration stops for a moment, as the story focuses on the drawings. Bruno walks around the marketplace with hopeful eyes and drooping ears. His movements are choppy, never smooth, but I still think I did a good job animating him.

"Bruno searched the city streets, and the tall buildings . . ."

On-screen, Bruno is pictured running down the rain-slick Seattle sidewalks. Pedestrians avoid Bruno, shielding their faces with their black umbrellas, stepping out of the way when he stops to shake the raindrops from his fur.

"Bruno searched the sandy beaches, and the public parks . . ."

On-screen, Bruno wanders through Golden Gardens. Bruno's too-enthusiastic tail knocks a plastic pail over in the sand, and accidentally levels an entire sandcastle. This time, a crowd of people start shooing the poor dog away from the beach, gesturing angrily with their hands. Bruno scampers off with his tail tucked between his legs.

Mom sighs beside me, sympathetic.

"Bruno was bullied and ostracized, alone and afraid. The city was a large and unforgiving place. Especially for those who seemed different. Especially for those who had no family, no community."

The graphite in the illustrations darkens to show that it's nighttime. Bruno curls up beneath an abandoned bench.

Uncle Phil points at the TV with his spoon. "These drawings are incredible, Edie."

I feel myself blush. "We haven't even gotten to

the colorful ones yet, Uncle Phil."

"Doesn't matter, kiddo. It's absolutely unbelievable that a couple of twelve-year-olds made this. You and Serenity will get a grand prize for this. Mark my words."

His words make me smile, even though prizes don't mean much to me. Sure, it would be cool if my work is recognized. But at the end of the day, I don't think I illustrated this short film to impress other people. More than anything, I just wanted my mom and my loved ones to see it.

And I want them to see how it ends. The ending is the part that matters most.

"Until one day," Serenity's voice narrates, *"Bruno found a ferry."*

On-screen, Bruno's surroundings brighten to signify the beginning of a new day. Bruno creeps out from underneath the bench, stretching his legs. He looks out at something in the distance with a cocked head.

The point of view switches to show the ferry, gliding across the bright blue water. In the distance beyond, the hills and mountains are visible.

The point of view turns back to Bruno, whose tail is wagging again.

"And Bruno thought, 'Maybe if I take the ferry, I'll find the people I've been looking for!'"

We watch as Bruno scurries down the winding road and boards the boat. The ferry begins its journey, and Bruno stretches up on his back legs, balancing his paws against the railing. His tongue lolls out the side of his mouth as the boat makes its way across the Puget Sound.

Except, instead of arriving in Kingston like it normally would, this one travels all the way to the historic site of Old Man House. *Except*, in this version of events, Old Man House was never destroyed. It never became a public park on the Agate Passage.

In our short film, Old Man House still exists. And Bruno has arrived, just in time for a huge potluck.

When Bruno joins the Suquamish and Duwamish families on the beach, the drawings finally shift to full color. The water becomes rich and blue, the trees turn green, the mountains in the distance are indigo. There are little kids and elders, people dressed in traditional regalia, and people dressed in sundresses and jeans and T-shirts.

My own family is there. Just like in Mom's

birthday card, our presence is obvious.

"*And that was how Bruno found his way home!*"

The screen fades to black.

Everybody sets their cake slices aside to applaud as the screen fades to black, even though the film technically isn't over. We still have the dedication left.

Within seconds, it appears:

This film was created in loving memory of
Edith Graham
(1952–1992)
Gone, but never forgotten

And that's when the tears fill my eyes.

I can't go back in time. I can't undo the wrong things that were done. I can't give her the roles she wanted. I can't ever write her a letter. I can't even let her know how proud I am to be named after her.

But I can give her this dedication. I can make this promise: that she might be gone, but she will never be forgotten.

Mom whispers, "That was beautiful, Edie."

They all come to me, hugging me and embracing me. My parents, my uncle, my best friend.

And in this moment, I feel so full. So full and loved and sure of myself.

I finally know where I'm from. And I'll carry this place and these people with me, wherever I go.

AUTHOR'S NOTE

As the daughter of a Native American Upper Skagit/Nooksack/Blackfeet/Nez Perce adoptee, I drew inspiration from my own life and my family's history while writing this book. I also gathered information from a variety of other sources. There are several references to real-world events, people, and places within these pages.

Sacheen Littlefeather is one famous example. She was the first person to ever give a political speech at the Academy Awards, though many activists have followed her lead since then. In the documentary *Reel Injun* (2009), Sacheen candidly reflects on her experience at the Oscars, and the impact this speech had on her life and career.

The demonstrations at Wounded Knee and Fort Lawton—which Uncle Theo fictionally participated in—were also real. The goal of the siege of Fort Lawton was to establish an urban center for Seattle's Native population, which had grown in the aftermath of Relocation and Termination policies in the 1950s. The Daybreak Star Indian Cultural Center exists today because of these efforts. The United Indians of All Tribes Foundation was granted a ninety-nine-year lease from the City of Seattle; hopefully this agreement will be renewed and supported for future generations.

The proposed Pebble mine at Bristol Bay is never directly addressed in this novel. However, through Edie's conversations with Uncle Phil, his backstory as a commercial fisherman in Alaska, and the salmon motif within the text, it feels important to mention the fight to protect the Bristol Bay watershed. A coalition of Alaska Native communities, commercial fishermen, sport fishing and hunting organizations, chefs and restaurant owners, churches, environmentalists, etc. all stand together in opposition to the Pebble mine. To learn more about their collective actions throughout the 2010s, please visit: www.savebristolbay.org.

Furthermore, the tribal nations mentioned throughout this book all exist. Almost all of them belong to the Coast Salish region, and have lived and thrived in the Pacific Northwest since time immemorial. Some are federally recognized, while others have been stripped of that status, due to broken treaties and legal complications. If you live in the Seattle area, it's possible you live in occupied Duwamish lands. To learn more and show your support for the People of the Inside, please visit: www.duwamishtribe.org. I would also recommend viewing the documentary films *Princess Angeline* (2010) and *Promised Land* (2016).

Old Man House was also a real place. Archaeological investigations support the deep histories of this site, as described and shared within Coast Salish societies. The longhouse was destroyed in 1870, and its residents were harshly displaced; Suquamish members rebuilt their village and lived there for a short while after the burning, but the government had other plans. The jurisdiction changed over the years—with allotments among

Suquamish families in the late 1800s, to the US War Department in 1904, to private developers, and to the Washington Parks and Recreation Department. This land wasn't formally returned to the Suquamish Tribe until August 12, 2004.

The procession of canoes in Chapter 34 was inspired by the Tribal Canoe Journeys, an annual tradition among Native Nations of the Pacific Northwest. The modern revival of these Canoe Journeys began in 1989, with the "Paddle to Seattle" in honor of the Washington State Centennial Accord. Each year, Native Nations from the coastal areas of Alaska, British Columbia, and Washington participate. The canoes travel to multiple locations throughout the region, before converging at a final host destination. In 2009, the Suquamish Tribe hosted the Canoe Journey in their House of Awakened Culture, where they welcomed over six thousand guests.

The Indian Child Welfare Act of 1978 is a vital piece of legislation. It helps to keep Native families and communities intact, after generations of forced removal. The goal of these coerced adoptions was to assimilate Native people into American society, at the expense of tribal nations. Almost all of the adoptees experienced the loss of their cultures, their identities, and the complex relationships that build the foundation of Native societies.

In the article "Native Americans Expose the Adoption Era and Repair Its Devastation," which was written by Stephanie Woodard and published in *Indian Country Today*, the following was stated: "During the adoption era almost any issue—from minor to serious—could precipitate the loss of an Indian child. Two Native people interviewed . . . said they were separated from their families after hospital stays as young children, one for a rash, the other for tuberculosis. A third was seized at his babysitter's home; when his mother tried to rescue him, she was jailed, he said. A fourth recalled that he was taken after his father died, though his mother did not want to give him up. A fifth described being snatched, along with siblings, because his grandfather was a medicine man who wouldn't give up his traditional ways." These real-life examples illustrate only a few of the reasons why Native children might have been transferred into adoptive homes or foster care.

It is my sincere hope that the ICWA will never be repealed.

ACKNOWLEDGMENTS

Typing the word *Acknowledgments* in Microsoft Word is so surreal. I must apologize in advance for the excessive exclamation points. I'll try to rein myself in, but I'm an extremely excitable and emotional person, so I can't make any promises! (Hah!)

To Rosemary Brosnan: When Suzie told me *you* made an offer on my manuscript, I had to pinch myself. I'm *still* pinching myself. Thank you for seeing some potential in a newbie like me, and for believing in Edie's story from the start. You make me feel like a braver and more capable writer. I'm so grateful for your kindness, your great laugh, and your brilliant mind. I'm learning from the best of the best!

And to everyone else at HarperCollins Children's Books: a million thanks for the million things that happen in the publication process. Courtney Stevenson, you brighten my inbox. Ann Dye, Emma Meyer, and Olivia Russo, thank you for working so hard to help Edie find her audience. Patty Rosati and Rebecca McGuire, thank you for being fantastic brunch companions, and also for bringing my book into schools and libraries. Kristen Eckhardt, Laura Harshberger, and Gweneth Morton, thank you for overseeing the production process. Sarah Kaufman, your design work is truly visionary. Thank you for everything. Edie found an excellent home with all of you!

To Michaela Goade (Tlingit): Your cover art is a deeply cherished gift. I wrote an entire blog post about it, so you already know how much I love it. I raise my hands to you. Thank you!

To Suzie Townsend: I'm absolutely convinced that I have the best agent in the business. Thank you for championing my work, for celebrating every milestone, and for the wonderfully random topics we discuss sometimes. (Like the sheep in Iceland! And the stuff about *Twilight*!) You make my wildest dreams come true.

Additional thanks go to Suzie's former assistant, Sara Stricker, who plucked my little manuscript out of the slush pile. And big, big thanks to everyone else at New Leaf Literary!

To my parents: Mom, thank you for encouraging me to write a story loosely based on our experiences. I couldn't have done this without your permission and enthusiasm. Dad, thank you for always believing I'd make it as a published author. I might have dedicated this book to the mothers and grandmothers, but I hope you know this one's for you, too. I love you both. Thank you for raising me and supporting me in everything I do.

To my sister: Like a pile. (Inside joke.) Love you, Jen!

To my husband: I love you so much, Mazen! Thank you for seeing me the way I want to be seen, and for keeping me sane and steady when I need a deep breath, or a cup of coffee. Every word I write is actually a love letter to you. Thank you for challenging me when I settle into my comfort zone for too long. Thank you for reminding me that life should be fun, when the stress starts to compound. Thank you for making me laugh, every single day. Thank you for agreeing to be my partner in everything.

To my in-laws: Mado, Elias, Christina, Josh, my nieces. I'm so lucky to have you guys in my life! Thank you for your warmth and love and unconditional support over the years.

To Dr. Luana Ross and Daniel Hart: I'm indebted to you both. Thank you for helping me reconnect with Native communities in really big, tangible ways. Thank you for mentoring me, and for presenting me with intellectual challenges and new ways of thinking. (Or new to me, at least!) And of course, for being the officiants at my wedding. You were brilliant.

To the University of Washington Department of American Indian Studies: I met so many wonderful folks in grad school. Special thanks to Dr. Christopher Teuton, Cynthia Updegrave, and Elissa Washuta for the field trip to the historic site of Old Man House. And to Ed Carriere, the Suquamish Elder who hosted us there. As I'm sure you can tell—given the contents of this book—that trip made a big impression on me. Thank you for teaching me to find ancient roots and sacredness in seemingly contemporary, colonized spaces. I would also like to thank Virginia Adams and Danielle Morsette, two Suquamish weavers who met with me when I was working on my thesis. I'm so grateful for your time, your generosity, and your wisdom. I also visited two weavers from the Squamish Nation, Skwet-simeltxw Willard "Buddy" Joseph and Chepximiya Siyam' Chief Janice George. Thank you for welcoming me into your home, and sharing your words with me. Lastly, I would like to recognize my small but mighty cohort from the Native Voices program, Tara and Rafa.

To the Coast Salish people of the past, present, and future: you lift me up.

To everyone involved with #DVpit: Beth Phelan, thank you for creating this wonderful event. I'm grateful to the agents I interacted with through this experience, and the kind folks who have urged me on from the moment they heard Edie's pitch.

To the Novel Nineteens: we made it, friends! High fives all around.

To my other author friends: Amy Reed, thank you for bringing me in. Cynthia Leitich Smith, thank you for seeking me out and making me feel so welcome. Somaiya Daud, I'm so glad the universe kept urging me to meet you. Amanda Lovelace and Cyrus Parker, thank you for years of friendship and beta reads. You two will always have your Octobers, and I'm so happy I got to be there for at least one of them.

To all my other friends and family members: You know who you are. Thank you for being in my life. Sending you all lots of love, always.

And to everyone else who has guided me—knowingly or unknowingly—through this process: Thank you!